To Colleen

Spooky Tales and Scary Things

2

Harry Carpenter

First published by Midnight Destiny Publishing 2020

Copyright © 2020 by Harry Carpenter

All rights reserved. No part of this publication may be reproduced, stored or transmitted in any form or by any means, electronic, mechanical, photocopying, recording, scanning, or otherwise without written permission from the publisher. It is illegal to copy this book, post it to a website, or distribute it by any other means without permission.

This novel is entirely a work of fiction. The names, characters, and incidents portrayed in it are the work of the author's imagination. Any resemblance to actual persons, living or dead, events or localities is entirely coincidental.

First edition
ISBN: 978-1-7344634-2-2

Dedicated to my wife, who has to hear about these crazy stories. And to my grandparents for having such history-filled stories and experiences to pass on.

"Believe nothing you hear, and only one half that you see."
— Edgar Allan Poe

Introduction

Hey, and welcome back for a few more short stories of things that creep me out. If you read Spooky Tales Number one, you'd know that each story is personal. Each one, in some fashion, happened to me. I just wanted to take the time to thank you, the reader, for checking out these stories. Book One was full of demonic entity-based stories, whereas Book Two will be nothing but ghost stories. Who am I kidding? What book of mine wouldn't be complete without some crazy demon story?

One of the more exciting things I've learned in my journey of horror is how receptive to the spirit world my family is. On my father's side, relatives have shared stories about being sensitive to the spirits and seeing, feeling, and even communicating with the other side. I started to do some digging into this. Through the family tree, I discovered that someone somewhere has some story or encounter that they shared with their children, passing it down through the generations. From apparitions to shadows, they all saw or felt something.

I'm a person of fact. I like tangible things to understand. If I can't see, feel, or understand it, I'm not a fan. Religion is one of the big ones for me. I'm sure there is something after we pass away, but no one has seen it. On that same token, the spirit world feels the same way. The millions of shows on television that ghost hunt always crack me up. I never believe anything they are "feeling" because I can't feel it through the TV. The guys with their cameras and tech jumping at every noise or whisper always fascinate me. I've never really had any experience to justify what happened. I even had one such occasion debunk my feelings further.

Some friends and I went off to some burned-down all-girls school or something back in the day. I don't recall the name, but it wasn't too far from where I was living at the time. The story goes that it was haunted, of course. The four of us trekked out there to check out what the hoopla was about. I'll admit, the building, or what was left of it, was ominous and foreboding. It was scary as shit, to say the least. It didn't warrant me jumping to conclusions about it being haunted, however. We cruised around what was still standing, finding nothing. Nothing popped out to get us. Short of my mind playing tricks on me, nothing eventful happened. It was a waste of a ghost hunt, as far as I was concerned.

Fast forward to the current day. About a year or so ago, I went on a ghost hunt. I may have mentioned I volunteer with a group of people who dress like the 1984 film Ghostbusters. We do charities and other fun events, and a ghost hunt was right up our alley. We went along, mostly being eye candy for the event. We visited the Lord Baltimore Hotel, reportedly one of the most haunted places in the state, if not the country. We meandered around and talked to the staff. We heard stories about a little girl who died from the rooftop. We heard about businessmen apparitions that floated the halls—the usual bunch of stories you'd expect to find with a place this old.

After we heard about the papers blowing off tables and people seeing shadows in the halls, we moved on to the hunt. We were broken down into groups of a dozen or so people. Each team member of ours got to break off in pairs with a group of tourist ghost hunters that signed up for the tour. Having that many people involved obviously would scare off any chance of encountering something anyway. We went along and found nothing. The spirit box was the most unsettling part of the night but really wasn't conclusive.

We retired back to the giant ballroom to perform one final massive group spirit box session. They had a psychic medium and all the gadgets doing something investigative. A few of our group and I found themselves tucked away in a corner waiting for the night to end. One of our guys is an actual ghost hunter himself and brought along a little toy to play with. It's basically a giant dictionary of words that the ghosts can pull from and communicate. For example, if Bob Smith died and he was a firefighter, the words "emergency" or "response" could be significant, as well as the word "firefighter." The problem is the term "firefighter" would likely never come up, and you'd probably come to the idea that "emergency" appearing on the screen was ol' Bob trying to speak to you from the grave.

As I said before, I think this stuff is a bunch of bull. All of my experiences have been my own brain getting in the way. Even if I think I saw something, I ruled it out as my brain being stupid. The human brain is a fickle thing. Something this night changed me entirely. We knew one of our former team members, David, was a massive fan of this hotel. He always said he'd love to investigate it and would likely haunt it when he passes away.

With that said, Steve, our ghost hunter guy, was fiddling with the library of words program. He jokingly tried to communicate with our late friend, David. The term

"British" came across the screen. Now I know that sounds out there in left field for a result, and it's garbage, right? Wrong. David was British. I was paying attention now. I awaited the next set of letters to hit the screen. The words "books" popped up. I told him that this app was garbage and a waste of time. It just rolled the dice on British and got lucky.

"Wait. We went to the comic convention today and sold David's Star Wars book collection!" Steve told me.

I paused for a moment. I wasn't sure how to correctly handle this one. Maybe we were putting the pieces together the way we wanted them to fit. Or, perhaps, this thing was working. There was only one way to find out.

"Ok. If you're David, go over to their voice box machine and say an obscenity. Say 'penis' or something. Loud and clear. I need to hear it and watch that nice old lady write it on her paper," I said out loud to nobody.

Nada. Absolutely nothing. I didn't hear one bit of vulgarity over the static-filled air. The whole thing was a complete and total bullshit waste of time. It was a waste, that is, until Steve showed me the device once more.

"Nuts."

It said nuts. Ok, I'll bite. Maybe the dictionary program didn't have penis in the list, but nuts may have been the closest thing? I'm still not sold on the idea of us communicating with our dead friend, but I'm listening. We waited until the ghost session had finished up, and I approached the spirit medium. She was a nice older lady and would have no reason to bullshit us. I also wanted to be as vague as humanly possible with my description and details of everything.

"Hey, fun story," I started, "our friend passed away not long ago, and, for some reason, we believe he haunts this hotel."

The medium hesitated for a moment before speaking. She acted as if what she was going to say was sensitive. Steve and I waited patiently for her response.

"I did feel a new spirit here, on the fourth floor. A spirit kept saying to me, "I'm sorry. I'm sorry" repeatedly. Did he take his life?"

I froze. I didn't say he killed himself. I said he passed away. There are a billion and one ways you could go. Heart attack, car wreck, even mauled by a lion. She hit the nail on the head. Lucky guess, I suppose.

"Did he hang himself? He was very remorseful and apologetic."

Her last statement hit hard because that was absolutely what happened. I called the group over. After she repeated what she said, we all were floored. *Could he actually be here?* We asked to borrow some ghost toys and headed to the fourth floor. We scanned around, finding nothing but a decent Wi-Fi signal from the army of routers on the ceiling. I decided to tap into Steve's toy once more.

"London."

The system gave another British-related clue. Still not conclusive enough for me. We walked away a bit shaken by the whole thing, but no worse for wear. We dropped off the gadgets and said our farewells. One of our team members was going to stay behind for a bit with his son. He went off to talk to the ghost hunters. We headed to our cars and never looked back.

I received a text around one in the morning. It was Ross, the guy who stayed behind to enjoy the afterparty of the investigation. He said he spoke to the other psychic—the one who could see actual physical manifestations of the spirits. Again, I thought it was some hokey garbage. Through our group text, he said something that was an absolute game-changer for all of us.

"Hey, I talked to the psychics. The lady that could see stuff saw David. He was watching from the balcony of the ballroom we were in," the text read.

One of us replied with the obligatory 'What!' before he continued.

"She said she saw a guy on the balcony wearing a very nice, dapper suit. He had a long coat on top of it. The people she sees are typically a blur, but she could make out enough. He seemed middle-aged and to be smiling at the group."

He then told us that he showed her a picture from the Facebook of David, dressed as Doctor Who. The psychic nearly came to tears.

"Yes. That's exactly who I saw. That's almost what I think he was wearing!" the psychic said, obviously startled.

We all determined that perhaps ghosts may or may not exist, but we cannot dismiss the experience we all had that night. Maybe it was the concentrated energy of all of us in the same building? Perhaps the Lord Baltimore is really haunted? Is it possible ghosts are real? After that experience, I'm leaning more towards yes.

Thank you for listening to my story! One heck of an opening, am I right? It's almost like a fourth story for my three-story collection, but I felt I should preface my thoughts and feelings towards ghosts in the past with how I feel about it now.

Spirits in the Attic

One after another, I watched the white lines on the road pass under the hood of the car. It had been hours since I pulled over at a rest stop, and I was about due to find somewhere for the night as it was. The trip I was taking was one for inspiration and clarity. You see, I needed to clear my head after my last book. It was a real doozie, and true crime can sometimes take its toll on your psyche. I wasn't immune to the research, the study, and the mental state I would find myself in after hours of writing. They don't teach you that in school.

My latest hit had taken me on a book tour across the states. It was a nice reprieve from sitting alone in my den by the fireside, trying to come up with comprehensible words to type. Truthfully, I always saw these as a vacation and not work, per se. Meeting new people, seeing new sites, it never felt like a chore to me. I was a short few hours from my next bookstore, but the night crept in on me faster than I was ready for. I stopped off at a local Best Western for the evening. I grabbed my small backpack of belongings and headed inside to the front desk.

"All booked up, sir!"

The clerk exuded such positivity that it was nauseating as well as excessively exhausting. I didn't even reciprocate a response to the clerk. I turned and left without a word. *No vacancy.* How does a vast several-story building fill up in the middle of October? Probably some lousy event taking place nearby that was causing the influx of bookings. I still needed to find something and quick. I pulled my laptop from my bag and attempted to connect to the hotel Wi-Fi. I was unsuccessful, of course. They only give this out with the booking of a room. I should have known.

I opted to try to figure out the next best thing: to find a restaurant or fast-food establishment that offered wireless Internet connectivity. I needed to find somewhere to stay the night. I took the car down what I assumed was the main road, scanning either side for anything of worth. I must have gone another seven or eight miles down the road before I found a small diner on the right. It was some local joint, but I was hopeful they were at least in the modern age. I parked the car and made my way inside.

The Monarch Diner, as it was named from the signage on the outside, did not disappoint. The interior was full of butterfly design work. The floor was stylized in the wing pattern. The seatbacks at the bar section were all butterfly wings. I was disgusted and impressed at the same time. It seemed to be the right place to grab a bite to eat, so I may as well roll the dice and see how it plays out.

"Seat yourself, hun," the waitress called from beyond the bar area.

I selected a booth in the far corner, away from everyone. I didn't want to get wrapped up in the local riff-raff if I had the chance to avoid it. Once I settled in, the laptop came out. Once it fired up, every head turned on a swivel in my direction. One by one, the patrons went back to their meals and conversation. I never felt like more of an outsider in my whole life. Such is the life of the weary traveler, I assume. I don't know why they were staring at me, considering they were the ones sitting in butterfly-shaped seating.

The menus were kept on the table near the sugar and ketchup in a butterfly-shaped file holder. I can't stress enough how overboard this place went with the design theme. I applaud them on the dedication, though.

"Coffee?" the waitress asked as she approached my table with a steaming pot of brew.

"Coke, please," I said as I continued to stare at the menu.

The waitress stood there for a few moments. I didn't know what the heck she was standing there for, but it made me uncomfortable. I glanced up from my menu to see what the problem was.

"Pepsi products. Pepsi ok, hun?" she huffed, half scowling at me.

I realized I had been rude and ignoring her. I'm not used to being around people or really communicating with people on this level. Back home, the shop I frequented knew my order—crepe with ham, pepper jack cheese, and egg. I also always had a Coke. Paul knew how to handle my order, for sure. I hated going to new places for this very reason. They also didn't give dirty looks at the crepe shop for writing my books, either.

"Pepsi is fine."

I could tell my tone wasn't that of *fine*. I came off as rude, rash, and, quite frankly, an asshole. I packed my laptop into my backpack and headed for the restrooms. I didn't want to leave my expensive electronics full of half-finished stories out for anyone to steal. I passed by a jukebox as I rounded the corner to the restrooms. I glanced at some of the selections, noticing it was full of the classics. After taking a much-needed leak and splashing some water on my face, I was ready to face the world. I towel dried my face and disposed of the paper in the bin before exiting.

I returned to my seat to find a Pepsi already staged for me. Looking at the menu once more, I settled on a Rueben. It seemed the safer of the options that they offered, although all-day breakfast was tempting. After a few moments of thumbing through her tickets, the waitress came back to my table.

"Ready yet, hun?" she asked with a hint of annoyance in her tone.

"Yes, actually. I wanted to apologize for earlier." I said, closing the menu. "I have been on the road for hours. I didn't mean to come off brash."

"It's fine. What are you eating, hun?"

"Well," I looked at the nametag, "*Doris.* Doris, I'll take the Reuben and a side of fries. I'm Banks. Tony Banks."

Doris looked at me as if she should know me or understand why she would even care about my name. I guess she never heard about my books. Not many people would know a writer in person these days anyhow. Nowadays, it's all about movie stars and reality TV personalities. They'd recognize them in a heartbeat. Writers never really get much facetime with the public. Honestly, I liked it that way. I wasn't mobbed by the paparazzi in the restroom at inopportune times.

I decided to pen down a new story. I was working on a southern gothic supernatural thriller. I hadn't keyed one word to date, but I had the description typed in my word processor. I stared blankly at the blinking cursor that followed 'written by Tony Banks.' How the hell was I supposed to start this, anyhow? Dark and stormy night? A day like any other? I didn't want the cliché fodder to spew out from my fingertips. I needed something new. What would it be, I wondered?

After getting lost in my thoughts for too long, my food had arrived. Thankfully, It looked appetizing and hot. To be honest, I wasn't really sure what to expect with a small-town diner. The taste matched the visuals. Everything was cooked to perfection, including the fries. I barely needed to coat them in ketchup, which was rare. Whatever oil they fried the food in was different. I just hoped it was clean and not what I was dreading, which was dirty oil filled with contaminants.

With each bite of my Rueben, I stared longingly at the blinking cursor. It practically caused me anxiety to see it anymore. I needed to face the reality that I was dealing with a bout of the dreaded writer's block. I knew it would get me one day. Why today? Biting into my Rueben once more, I mulled around a loose plot involving a retired cop that teams up with the ghost of his partner to find his killer. After taking a sip of my soda, I was sure that the story had been done before. I moved on to the next brilliant idea my brain could cook up.

"Refill, hun?" Doris asked as she passed by my table.

My soda was empty, and I hadn't noticed. I nodded, face full of food. Doris whisked away my glass and headed toward the kitchen. I needed something for inspiration. A location, a person, anything. Maybe Doris? Yeah, I could do something with her. I bet she's a good character who likely has seen something ghostly in a southern restaurant I could use. *Christ, am I really fishing for ideas this bad?* While I daydreamed, Doris had dropped off my full glass of Pepsi.

I wrapped up eating and requested the bill from Doris. She promptly pulled it from her apron and dropped it face down on the table.

"You can pay at the counter, hun," she said as she collected my empty plates from the table.

I shut down my laptop and packed up for the night. I headed to the front counter to pay, only to be greeted by Doris once more. I guess they did all of the work at this place. I handed a twenty-dollar bill and the ticket to Doris to check out.

"Know anywhere nearby to stay at?"

Doris paused from pressing the buttons on the cash register.

"Well, if I may offer a suggestion, and you want to hear it, I know a place," she replied.

I was interested to hear her suggestion. I figure the locals knew the hotels that don't get booked up.

"There's a bed and breakfast about two miles off the highway from here. They usually have vacancies and could likely take you in. Even at this hour." She drew some register receipt tape from the dispenser and wrote down something on it. "It's a few minutes up the road. Cheryl will take good care of you. It's an old house too, full of charm."

Doris slid the register tape to me with an address scrawled onto it. She also included basic instructions on how to get there from the diner. Doris finished cashing out my bill and handed me back nine dollars and change. I reached into my wallet to grab another five and put it with the nine. I gave it to Doris.

"Hun, you don't have to do that much. You were an easy customer," she said, pushing the handful of cash back toward me.

I pushed the money forward once more. "I insist."

She took the fourteen-dollar tip, which was more than my total order, and placed it into her apron.

"Good luck on the road, sir!" Doris said with a wave as I made my way out the door to the car.

The road ahead wasn't too tricky to navigate. It was a clear night, and not a car in sight—my kind of driving conditions, to be honest. I followed the instructions to the mark. Stop at the sign three streets up. Turn right. Drive until you see the blinking yellow light overhead. I took the leftmost road, bearing off the main road to that of a gravel path. It was a driveway, not paved but not unkempt. I felt the tiny rocks crackle and crunch under the tires.

Upon the hill, I was greeted by a sizeable Victorian-style home. These houses were beautiful and the obvious choice for most B&B owners. They had charm, history, and curb appeal. I parked in what I could deduce was the apparent parking area for patrons and headed toward the door. The front porch was covered and filled with wicker furniture. There was a lovely swing on the left end of the porch, which overlooked the valley below. The windows were painted with an off-white color, and the house was powder blue, as far as I could tell in the porch lighting. A rug greeted me at the doorstep that read, "Bless this house and all in it."

I rang the doorbell. I hoped that this wasn't too late for my soliciting their services. Ten at night was late for a small-time business, I thought. Just as I finally felt awkward enough to turn around to leave, I heard the deadbolt flick open. A few moments later, and with several locks clicking, the door creaked open. An Asian-American gentleman greeted me from behind the door.

"Hello, are you here for lodging for this evening?" he asked in a soft, clear tone. I partially expected an accent.

I nodded back to him in agreement.

"Ah, well, come in! Do you need to bring more baggage into the lobby?" he asked, noticing how empty-handed I arrived at the door.

I glanced behind me, eying up my car trunk from the threshold of the doorway. The caretaker pushed me onward to retrieve my bags and began to walk with me toward the car.

"I'm Wendell, by the way. Nice to meet you."

The rocks crunched and cracked under the soles of our shoes as we cut through the parking lot.

"Tony. Tony Banks, sir," I responded as I pulled the keys from my pants pocket to pop the trunk open.

The car trunk sprang open with ease, and Wendell reached in to grab my bags. I grabbed the backpack with my laptop in it and closed the trunk. Wendell and I turned and headed back for the home.

"First time in town?" Wendell asked.

"Yeah. Passing through."

"Oh, on your way to where?"

"Book signing. I have to be up and out early and about two hours north of here."

Wendell opened the door for me. He picked my bags back up and placed them in the foyer as we stepped inside.

"A writer! My oh my, that's entertaining. You know, I used to play piano back in my day."

I gave Wendell a look of interest so he would continue.

"I used to play in this house for all kinds of people. I used to professionally play as well. Did you know back in my youth, I opened for Elton John in the early eighties?"

"No shit," I exclaimed, somewhat surprised at his feat.

A door creaked closed to my left, causing me to jump nearly out of my skin.

"Now, who is using that foul language in my home?" a woman's voice asked.

A grey-haired, short woman with a small orange cat joined us in the foyer.

"Cheryl, this is Tony. He's going to be staying with us for the night. Can you check him in?" Wendell asked as he headed off down a hallway to my right.

Once I penned my autograph a few times on some paperwork, I was handed a key to a room.

"You're in room 102. Just keep in mind this is an old home, and you may hear creaks and groans. That's either the house settling or Wendell showing his age again," Cheryl said with a laugh.

I looked at the key. It was an old historical key. They don't make them like this anymore, I can tell you that. The Kwik-Key cutter at the hardware store doesn't make these. This is the kind of key you'd find in an antique store in an "assorted old keys" bin. It added to the charm. Doris was right; this would be a charming place.

I followed Cheryl up the stairs with my bags in hand. The stairs were lined with a gorgeous carpet that I almost felt guilty walking on with shoes. The chandelier that hung from the ceiling was mounted gracefully in the center of the spiral of the staircase. Fine art adorned the walls as we climbed to the second floor. Each room, the three of them, was marked with a room number marker on the center of the door. There were five doors in total, but only two had room numbers. I assumed one was at least a linen closet.

"Ok, Mr. Tony. This is your room right here," Cheryl said.

I tried the key in the door. It slid in and turned with ease, just like the day it was made. They really knew how to keep up a house, I'll tell you.

"If you need anything, just reach out to the front desk. Wendell works the night. I'll be turning in myself shortly," said Cheryl as she made her way back down the large staircase.

The door swung open rather silently. *They must oil the door hinges to keep this place as quiet as possible,* I thought to myself.

Entering the room, I noticed it was decorated in a red tone. The room itself was covered in a velvet-like wallpapering, tinted red. There was a king-size bed to my right and a bathroom just across from it. The room size was immaculate. Frankly, I was impressed by how large it was. A small tube TV rested on an armoire to the right of the bed. I turned it on low just to have background white noise. As I pulled out my clothing for the following morning, I kept having this strange feeling. The back of my neck felt warm.

I assumed my neck had that sensation because I had been in the car for the day. Maybe it was tension, and I needed to relax. I set out my slacks and button-down shirt over the armoire and checked out the bathroom. This room was done in a salmon-like pink color. I checked the shower out, as well as tested the sink. I'm not sure why I ran the water for a moment or two, but I did. I opted to take a quick shower to wash the drive off of me.

I retreated back to the bedroom to check that the lock was engaged in the door. Once secured in my room, I stripped off the clothing I was wearing, grabbed my soap and shampoo, and made my way to the shower. The water pressure was surprisingly intense. In most old homes, you find that you can barely get the water to dribble on you, let alone nearly blow the skin from your body. I set it to a lovely hot setting and washed away hours of car riding in five minutes.

Once finished, I turned the shower off and grabbed one of the towels on a shelf next to the tub—standard white linens. I still felt that warm sensation on my neck, and I figured I better take a look at it in the mirror. As I approached the mirror, a handprint was visible in the center. I couldn't remember if I touched the mirror coming in and chalked it up to an old greasy handprint from a previous guest or even the staff. I wiped away the steam from the mirror to see my neck. Nothing stood out from what I could tell. I figured it best to just get ready for some sleep.

I set my watch alarm to wake me at 8 AM. I figured that I can snooze for another thirty, wake up, and get ready and be out by 9. A stop for drive-thru breakfast on the way, and I'd be at the book store by noon at the latest, ready for my 1 PM signing. I was already sick of touring this book as it was, but the thought of my last stop on the tour made this so much more bearable. It would be nice to get back to my own house and see my personal belongings once again. I smiled at the thought as I climbed into bed. I turned off the lamp next to my bedside, only to see the room in a faint blue glow.

I had forgotten to turn off the television. I stared at it as it faintly muttered words from a television show I couldn't make out. I think it was Lucy or Green Acres. Heck, it could have been a new show, but I wouldn't have been able to tell. The picture was in black and white. This really was a relic inside of an antique. I sighed audibly enough for the world to hear my frustration and turned the television off. I decided to take a leak while I was up as well. I didn't need any more interruptions. Once completed, I returned again to the comfort of the bed.

The bed, blankets, and pillow were the perfect combination. I don't even remember my eyes closing or actually falling asleep. What I do remember was being woken up by the rudest of neighbors in this lovely B&B.

Thump. Thump. Thump.

I heard it loud and clear—a thumping sound. Some asshole is dragging their bag either up or down the stairs. I laid my head deeper into the pillow to ignore the sounds and go back to sleep. It was so hard to ignore.

Thump. Thump. Thump.

I didn't really feel like dealing with the Telltale Heart next door. If I heard any more thumping, bumping, or jumping, I was going to go give them a piece of my mind. Maybe I'd help them get their luggage to the appropriate floor by inappropriate means. Who knew?

Silence fell over the room once more. The thumping stopped. I no longer heard somebody's amateur rendition of Stomp outside—finally, peace and quiet. I glanced at my wristwatch. 1 AM. Great, I was barely asleep. I nestled my way back into a cozy spot to fall asleep once more. I felt myself drifting off to dreamland once more.

Thump. Thump. Thump. Thump. Thump.

This time, it was as if someone was running up the stairs or in the hallway. This was uncalled for. I felt my body grow angry enough to throw the covers from my body and reach for the lamp. I flipped the lamp on, and the room filled with an ominous blood-red glow. I threw on a pair of sweats I had stashed in a suitcase and made for the door. I was ready to kick someone's ass at the witching hour. I ripped open the door and stepped into the hall. The hallway was dimly lit as if set by a switch or timer for the hour. Most hotels remained brightly lit at all times. This place was not a hotel, that's for sure.

    I whirled my head around, trying to see who was making all of that noise. No doors were open—no overweight man with his nagging wife dragging suitcases upstairs or down. Not a single soul to be found. I figured I should at least check downstairs to see if someone was checking in or out at best. I made my way down the spiral staircase to the empty foyer. Not one person waited for me. Not even Wendell, who I assumed could also have been making the noises. Not likely, as they'd lose business that way quickly.

    I gave up my hunt and retreated back to my room. The door was half-open. I must not have closed it when I went on my crusade of ass-kicking. I grabbed the doorknob and thrust it open, and stormed into the room. I froze in place. A woman stood staring at the foot of the bed. She was staring at the spot where I would have been lying had I have been in it. I saw her clear as day, and then all at once—I didn't. I dramatically shook my head like a cartoon character who just ran into a wall to clear my head. I must be exhausted.

    I closed and locked the door behind me and did a quick search around the room, just in case. Everything seemed in order. I returned to the bed, keeping my sweats on in the event I needed to burst out of the room and implement a swift dropkick to the noisy neighbor. I turned off the lamp once more and closed my eyes to fall asleep. I listened carefully for any banging and thumping noises, but I was met with silence from the house. *Thank God.* I quickly felt myself fading away once more into my slumber.

In what felt like a matter of minutes, I heard a new noise. A shuffling, almost dragging sound. It was like a child dragging their feet across the carpet, ready to static shock the next unsuspecting victim. It was distinct and unmistakable; It was clear and coming from inside the room. I almost didn't want to open my eyes. I wasn't sure what I'd find, but I knew I'd have to. Slowly, I opened my eyes. The pale moonlight that shone into the room provided enough light to make out most of the room. I saw the stupid outdated television, the armoire, and my suitcases. Everything seemed almost normal.

The shuffling noise began again. I glanced to my left near the door and saw a figure moving toward the foot of the bed. I squinted as best I could until it stepped enough into the moonlight for me to see. It was that woman! There, at the foot of my bed, staring at me as she did before. She stood, motionless, soundless. I reciprocated the feeling and remained motionless and soundless myself. I believe I even shallowed my breaths because I didn't know who she was or why she was in my room. I thought it was Cheryl, but this woman seemed far too young to be her. Also, the hair was different. This woman was a completely new face I hadn't met.

I lay there, staring at the figure who apparated at the foot of my bed. My feet were still at the end of the bed, and I desperately wanted to move them closer to the rest of my body. I feared that moving my feet would disturb whoever this was. The woman turned slowly and started toward the bathroom before disappearing once more. As soon as I felt confident she was no longer in the room, I reached for the side table lamp. I flipped it on, illuminating the whole room in the sickly red glow of the wallpaper once more.

I sat up and absorbed my surroundings. There was no other person in this room. I must have hallucinated or had those daydream types of dreams— those lucid dreams I hear about. I climbed back out of bed once more, searching the room for signs of entry. The door was locked, as was the window. I clearly needed sleep. I checked the bathroom, only to turn up empty-handed. Part of me wished I found someone so I could eject them from my room properly. I decided to take a quick walk through the home to clear my head and calm down.

I headed out to the hallway, closing and locking the door behind me. I looked around the upstairs. I found nothing of interest except for the grand piano off to the side of the room. I decided to twinkle the last two keys of the keyboard before moving toward the stairway. I rounded the stairs, descending to the first floor. I didn't see Wendell anywhere, so I wandered toward the kitchen area. A sign affixed to the refrigerator posted that patrons were free to take a water or can of soda as a courtesy. I grabbed a Coke from the top shelf. I know I should have taken water, but it seemed like a waste of my options.

I popped the can and began drinking as I headed back toward the stairs. At the foot of the stairwell, I checked my wristwatch. 3:30 AM. Christ, I needed to get to bed. I was losing precious sleep time and still had a drive ahead of me. I opted to finish the can of soda downstairs. I wasn't sure what the policy was for food and drink in the room and didn't want to chance ruining something of value. I went back to the kitchen and dropped my can into the recycling bin. As the can settled with the rest, I heard a familiar noise.

Thump. Thump. Thump.

I rushed to the stairs once more to see who was playing games. I would catch them off-guard this time. By the time I reached the staircase, whoever was stomping was gone. They had moved back into the hiding spot once more. Defeated in my goal to find this prankster, I retired back to my room yet again. I grabbed the doorknob, which was still locked. I gripped the key from my pocket and unlocked my door. Slowly turning the knob, I entered my room cautiously.

Empty. The entire room was as I left it. I knew I was losing it and needed sleep. Yeah, sleep would fix the issue. I headed to the TV and turned it on, and muted the volume. I was going to use the television as a makeshift night light as best I could. At least it would pour more light into the room to see what's going on if I have another lucid dream. I climbed back into bed and turned the side table lamp off once more. No sooner than I laid my head on the pillow, I was fast asleep. Finally, rest at last.

I was woken from my sleep once more by a new noise. This time, it wasn't stomping or a door. I opened my eyes and didn't see a woman at the foot of my bed, either. This was a new noise, a creaking noise. It sounded like a shutter that wasn't closed properly, gently blowing in the breeze. The faint blue glow of the television helped illuminate the room nicely. Nothing stuck out from what I expected to see. The creaking noise I could deal with. Houses settling were a natural thing, and this was a house built in a bygone era, after all. I went back to sleep.

As I began to drift gracefully into dreamland, I felt something watching me. That feeling is unmistakable. It's almost as if there is a burning sensation on your body to the point you can feel the eyes on you. I slowly opened my eyelids, hesitant at first, afraid of what I might find. As I adjusted to the blue glow of the room, I began to pan around. There was nothing ahead of me, nor near the television. Dick Van Dyke was playing, albeit muted, which I turned my attention to. Some normalcy was warranted.

As I focused on the latest shenanigan Laura and Rob found themselves into, something caused my heart to race. That feeling returned. The sensation of being observed was palpable. Slowly, I turned my head toward the door once more. Within the frame, a woman stood, arched over slightly, her head drooped toward the floor. I had a feeling it was the same woman as before. I think she sensed I was watching her.

Before I could reach for a light, the figure began to walk toward me. It sounded as if she was trying to speak, only able to utter terrifying clicking noises as she did. She seemed completely void of color, a grey color, in fact. She shuffled closer to the left side of the bed, passing in front of the television as she did. As she moved, the shuffling sound from earlier was heard; clearly, she was the source. The dragging of the feet, the thumping noise; it was all her.

As I looked onward at the figure, she began to turn toward my direction. Her head never looking up as she did. I gripped tightly at the blankets as if they would be able to save me. The figure shuffled two or three steps toward me as I froze in fear, unable to reach for the light. I was sure the light would save me in some childish way. The figure stopped just short of halfway up the bed.

I blinked slowly. I didn't want to miss a fraction of what was going on. I immediately regretted my actions. As I reopened my eyes, the woman began to lift her head. It bobbled as she did so as if a puppet on strings where the puppeteer let the marionette droop a bit. Her face was indiscernible, faded, and unrecognizable. I looked on as she inched closer to the bed.

The eyes. One thing I can never forget would be the eyes; soft, pale green. It was the only thing that seemed remotely reminiscent of a past she may have known. As I gazed into her eyes, her expression changed. Immediately, she began to weep, her body convulsing as she screamed a sound I don't believe I've heard from another human being in my life. As if in mockery of the struggle it took her to get to my side of the bed, she quickly reversed, walking backward as her body jerked and convulsed.

Once she exited the room, I heard the dragging sound again. It sounded more consistent this time as if sweeping back and forth. Exhaustion took hold of me, and I cannot recall the next few moments. I could hear crying. A bellowing sob that I never wish to hear again so long as I may live. The crying faded as I fell fast asleep.

My wristwatch began to beep. I reached for it, turning off the alarm—8 AM on the dot. I was wide awake, ready to remove myself from this place as quickly as possible. I promptly packed my loose belongings into my bags, making my way downstairs. I had a rough night of sleep. I may have left the television running in my haste, but I'm sure housekeeping would sort it out.

"Hello, Mister Tony. Did you sleep well?" Cheryl asked as I approached the small check-in table.

I think she could tell by my overall expression and appearance things did not go well.

"Oh, my. I can tell something is off. Did the room not treat you well?" she asked.

I hesitated. I didn't want to tell her I couldn't sleep because of someone banging something on the stairs or that a ghost was watching me sleep. She'd think I was crazy.

"Did Alice visit you last night, Mister Tony?" she asked casually.

My expression shifted. I was tired and groggy but quickly became all ears.

"I'm surprised Wendell didn't tell you! Goodness gracious, me. Where do I begin?" Cheryl said. "It all happened back in the late 1800s, well before we owned this home. A young lady by the name of Alice lived in this home with her family. The story says she met a nice boy, fell in love, and became pregnant with his child. Unfortunately, the relationship didn't work out, and he moved on. Alice didn't move on and remained heartbroken in this home. Eventually, she miscarried the child. It was so sad, and I couldn't imagine what she felt."

Cheryl spoke this story as sincerely as she could. I paid complete attention. My jaw dropped in shock.

Cheryl continued. "She walked up and down the stairs, pacing the home, awaiting the day her love would come back to her. He never returned. The rumors around town spoke ill of her. You see, back then, it was bad to be unwed with child or to have a miscarriage."

"Yeah, I can't imagine," I interjected, trying to seem like I understood life in the 20th century.

Cheryl finished signing out the last of the documents for the stay. She folded my hand receipt and placed it in an envelope with a brochure of the B&B in it. The envelope was slid across the counter to me, which I grabbed and tucked into my back pocket.

"So, what happened to her?" I asked, wanting to know what transpired with this poor woman.

"Oh, it was so sad, dear. Here was poor Alice, heartbroken, childless, friendless, and had nothing more to go on for. Her parents were ousted from social circles and disowned her. She had no siblings to speak of, either. Alice was the definition of alone," Cheryl said, almost fighting back a tear or two of her own. "Poor dear took her life not soon after."

My expression shifted to that of an awkward one. "May I ask how, if you know?"

"Poor thing hung herself. Before the remodel, the bathroom in your very room used to be part of the bedroom of young Alice."

A chill went up through my spine. I felt the heat once more on the back of my neck. My whole body felt uncomfortable. I needed to get the hell out of this place right away.

"Well, Cheryl, I'd love to stay, but I have to leave. I have to be at my book signing soon," I said, preparing to step toward my bags.

"Would you happen to have a copy of your book for Wendell and me? We will put it into the library in the den for guests to read."

Harry Carpenter

I put my bags into my car and returned with a signed copy of my true crime novel, "Webs We Weave and Spiders We Dream." I handed it to Cheryl, who thanked me gratefully for the book. I hauled ass, driving as quickly as I could down the dirt road. I made it to my book signing with time to spare and stopped at a fast-food restaurant for a quick bite.

I brought my laptop with me, booting it up once I had my food. I stared once more at the blinking cursor that followed the working title of my next book before pressing backspace on the description I jotted down for myself. I cracked my knuckles and penned the description and a working title for my next book, "The Gray Lady," before packing up everything and heading to my signing.

What is the real story?

Ok, so this is a journey that dates way back to the late 90s, early 2000s. I had been dating a girl whom I eventually married then divorced soon after. I wrote a whole other book about that one. When it started, she lived in a sizeable Victorian-era home in Baltimore. The house was broken off into different apartments on each floor, showing how large it actually was. I had been invited over for dinner and to stay the night. I packed my bags and made my way up to her house in her parents' car.

Everything was normal. I'd been in the house before, briefly. I mainly stayed on the ground level, exploring the den, kitchen, and dining room areas. I was having a blast after dinner. We played Super Smash Bros, walked the neighborhood, and enjoyed ourselves. Around 9, we began to settle down for the night. My girlfriend's father said I had to stay in the fourth-floor apartment. This was practically the attic at this point, but I was ok with it. I grabbed my belongings and made my way up several flights of old wooden stairs.

Nothing was out of the ordinary. The place came equipped with wall-to-wall carpeting, kitchen, and bathroom.

The bedroom was of a standard size for what I would assume would be an average bedroom. I turned off some of the lights, went to the restroom, turned the remaining lights off, and retired to my bed. The soothing sounds of police sirens lulled me into sleep.

    I was woken up at some point by a loud thumping, as I described in the story. The very same "thump, thump, thump" that I mentioned was stomping its way up and down the stairwell. I flipped on the light on the nightstand. Slowly, I made my way to the attic door that led to the stairs. Her father deadbolted the latch and locked it up so I couldn't sneak down and initiate any hanky panky. The funny thing was, the door was wide open! I didn't see anyone on the stairs, and the noise stopped. I assumed her younger brother was being an ass and went back to bed after locking the door from the inside.

    Maybe an hour or so later, the bumping came again. I went through the same process, only to find the door unlocked once more. I must not have latched it correctly and went about my night by locking the door again, double-checking that it held. As I headed back to the bedroom, something caught my eye. In the kitchen, someone was standing near the stove. This person was in front of me, picture-perfect. It wasn't until I focused more, I noticed they were facing me, watching and staring. I flipped on a nearby light only to find the kitchen completely empty. I needed to sleep.

    The next time I was woken up, there was a dragging sound. It sounded like someone in slippers scooting lazily across the floor, shuffling their feet across the carpet. I was about to kill her little brother if he didn't stop screwing around. I sat up in bed, forgetting to flip the side table light on. I could make out a figure slowly walking past my bedroom doorway, headed from the kitchen toward the main living room area in the shadows. The room was unfurnished, so traveling through this space posed no danger of smacking into a random table.

This was my moment. I was going to catch my girlfriend's brother messing around and make him wish he never popped that lock open. I threw the living room light on, only to be greeted by a hauntingly empty room—nobody standing in the center of the room any longer. I decided to leave the light on and went back to bed. I may have fallen asleep around three or four in the morning after forcing my eyes to close and ignoring what I saw.

The following day, I decided that what happened last night was a combination of a new environment mixed with a lack of sleep. I've spent the nights at friend's houses and felt as if I was being followed by something. I've felt it as well as in my own home. Of course, nothing has ever been there; it's my mind playing tricks on me. The door, still wide open, allowed my girlfriend and her mother to come upstairs undetected and scared the hell out of me in the room.

After calming down, I explained why I was so jumpy. Then my girlfriend's mother casually told me that there was a ghost in the attic. It was a young woman who tragically killed herself in the living room area before it was a finished room. She hung herself from the rafters after her husband left her for a servant or neighbor girl or something cliché like that. They seemed fuzzy about the exact details, but one thing was for sure: the girl walked through the living room that night.

I know I opened the book with the fact that I've been skeptical all my life. I still remained suspicious if this had been an elaborate hoax, and they were messing with me. Looking back at it now, I believe there was something in that attic. Someone that relived the tragic moment that they decided to take their own life, doomed to repeat the trauma for eternity: a terrifyingly sad tale, both fictional and real.

The Fall

Andrew never felt like he got enough sleep. It didn't matter what he did to wind down for the evening; he just couldn't fall asleep. His legs and arms would continue to work while his brain was in full gear. He tried just about everything. Andrew would sleep in absolute darkness, with a sleep mask to cover his eyes. He tried sleeping with the television on, but that only kept his interest in watching the good programs late at night. At one point, he opted for a white noise machine to give his room a soothing lull humming sound to put him to sleep. Nothing worked. He needed to seek out a professional.

A few sleepless nights later, he decided he was going to reach out to a sleep practitioner. Google was his best friend in trying to figure out who was nearby and what his insurance covered. Nothing turned up good results. They were either out of his insurance network or nowhere nearby for him to commute. Andrew felt like giving up. The sleepless nights were driving him absolutely insane. He searched up ways to go to sleep in the hopes that there was something he hadn't tried. He was hopeful for at least that much.

Lavender and chamomile, exercise, and something called "shutting off" were the top results he turned up. *Figures*, Andrew thought to himself as he moved away from his internet search and began scrolling endlessly through his FaceBook newsfeed. Post after post, status after status, he thumbed. The same formula, over and over. Photos of relationships, food, and pets were peppered throughout the text. The content bored Andrew to tears, but not enough to cause him to feel drowsy. He watched a new video from his favorite viral animal page to break up the scrolling pattern. Once it was finished, he resumed his regular motion, sliding his thumb across his smartphone repeatedly. A few swipes later, something caught his attention.

An advertisement flitted by his screen as he pushed onward down the column of updates. He moved back up to read it.

```
Trouble sleeping? Can't get a full
 8 hours? Can't even get a decent 6
 hours? Look no further! Click the link
  below to see what could change your
         life! *Not FDA Approved.
```

Andrew shrugged his shoulders. He stared at the blinking advertisement for a few moments before clicking the button to proceed to their website. Within the contents of the page were testimonials from doctors, clinical trials, and more. The more he read, the more convinced he became. At the top of the screen was a button that said: "Order Now." He clicked it. After entering several screens' worth of personal information, a bottle of this new miracle drug was on its way. A desperate time for a desperate man, Andrew let out a sigh of relief.

Two days later, the package arrived from the courier. It wasn't clearly marked, only labeled with his shipping address and a logo for BD Labs, the company that manufactured the product. It had no return address or other distinguishing marks on the box. Skeptical and suspicious, he placed the box on his coffee table in the living room, sitting across from it on the sofa. With his fingers pressed together, he rested his head on his fingertips.

"Hmm. So, I could take this and see how it goes. What's the worst that happens? I fall asleep?" Andrew said out loud to nobody in particular.

He picked up the box once again. It was a small six-by-six box. It was lightweight, feeling practically empty to the touch. Andrew pulled his keys from his pocket and tore at the shipping tape that held one end together. Inside was a folded half-sheet of paper and a bottle. He pulled the bottle out, setting it upright on the coffee table. The bottle was simply labeled "Sleep-Aid."

"That's not overselling the product at all," Andrew said as he reached for what he assumed were the instructions for the sleep aid.

He unfolded the sheet containing written instructions, side effects, and more. He began to read aloud.

"Sleep Aid is designed for those desperate enough to seek the most advanced treatment. Sleep Aid is a clinical trial drug not yet approved by the FDA. *Great, that's comforting.*"

He didn't see any markings other than the BD Labs logo in the top right corner. There wasn't a corporate headquarters listed in the header. He read the side effects.

"Known side effects include nausea, vomiting, sweaty palms, irritated stomach. In rare cases, patients have developed a small rash, easily treatable with a topical cream. Should any side effects not listed occur, please call this number immediately, and ask for Doctor Shatz. 1-800-555-9865. Good luck and sweet dreams!"

Andrew rubbed his temples after dropping the instructions on the table.

"What the hell am I about to do? Am I really doing this? I'm doing this," he said out loud once more to the empty room.

Andrew read the bottom corner of the paper containing instructions for the dosage.

Take 2 drops one hour before bedtime. The average time for activation is thirty minutes.

"Ok, so be in bed after I take it. Got it."

Andrew walked his bottle to the nightstand beside his bed and decided now was as good a time as any to give this new miracle juice a whirl. For being a small container full of liquid, it didn't weigh a thing. He hadn't broken the seal on the bottle just yet but felt he had been scammed with an empty bottle. Andrew stared at the potion, sitting on the edge of his bed.

"To heck with it. I'm doing it."

Andrew twisted the lid from the rest of the bottle, breaking the tape seal that secured the cap. Under the top was an attached dropper device. He removed the dropper and filled it with the mysterious liquid. Two drops were placed on his tongue, and he prepared himself for a good night's sleep. Capping the bottle, he turned off his lamp and climbed under the blankets. Within moments, he drifted off.

The following day, Andrew woke in his bed. He felt surprisingly refreshed, realizing he had slept the entire night. Sitting up from the bed, Andrew was greeted by a sharp pain on his torso. He leaned around to look, revealing a large bruise just under his arm on his right side.

"What the hell?" Andrew exclaimed to himself out loud.

He decided it best to venture off to the bathroom to get a better look at it. As he made his way out of the bed, Andrew noticed a few other bruises peppering his arms and legs.

One hell of a bad dream.

After checking himself out in the mirror, he was able to assess the damage. In contrast, a few bruises from a nightmare may have been worth the tradeoff for a night of restless sleep. Going to work was a breeze. He felt like his head was unclouded, and his energy renewed. No one questioned the bruises on his arms. After a successful day at work and a new lease on life, Andrew headed home.

Dinner and TV time felt like a new world to him. Rather than trying to fall asleep watching TV, he knew his medicine would take care of that issue. Day one was a success. By the time bedtime rolled around, Andrew was excited to go to sleep for the first time in ages. He retired to the bedroom, taking the proper two-drop dosage and falling asleep all the same once more.

The next morning, Andrew awoke with an uneasy feeling. His body ached more than it did yesterday.

"Must be more bruises," he said out loud.

He moved his arm to remove the blankets from his body. Instantaneously, he was immediately greeted by a sharp stabbing pain. He shrieked out loud in agony. Looking down at his arm, he noticed a large bruise as well as a new ailment, a broken bone. He'd broken bones in the past as a kid, so he was familiar with the pain and look. Nursing his arm and fighting back the tears, he carefully dressed and drove to the hospital. He called work from the waiting room, letting them know he wasn't coming in due to a broken arm. He was ready for the onslaught of questions to follow when he returned to duty.

The doctor saw Andrew soon after.

"So, how did we do this one? Skateboarding? Fight?" the doctor asked as he flipped through his chart.

"Sleeping," Andrew replied, slightly embarrassed.

The doctor stroked his chin for a moment, then resumed logging reports and data. This gave Andrew a bit of time to think about what was going on with him as well. This whole thing felt stupid. *Who breaks an arm sleeping in bed anyhow?* After being questioned by the doctor on vitamin intake, diet, and exercise, he was released after having the arm set in a cast. With his arm slung, he drove home to take a pain reliever and pass out.

Andrew sat on his sofa, turning the television to his favorite station. The pain reliever was the high-quality stuff, advising him to not take it with anything else. He felt it best to do just that. Restless, he lay awake watching television until four in the morning. He decided to get up and move around a bit, possibly make some breakfast with one arm.

He was miserable. After getting two nights of rest, regardless of the consequences, he felt he was missing out on something that had been abruptly taken away.

Moving toward the instructions for his bottle of sleep meds, he searched the paper for any type of ingredients or instructions for taking it with other medication.

"Technically, the doctor said to not take it with other medication. I don't think this is a medication. More of an herbal remedy type thing," Andrew said out loud as he tossed the instructions back on the table.

Working the pill bottle with his teeth and only good hand, Andrew pried the lid open. Filling the dropper, he squeezed a few drops onto his tongue, returning the dropper back to its bottle. Slumping back into the sofa, he returned to staring mindlessly at the television at the late-night programming he was tuned to. As the dialogue rolled on, it became more and more muffled as the minutes went by. Andrew felt more relaxed than ever.

Andrew awoke in an unfamiliar room. The walls were white, and there was an audible beeping sound surrounding him. As his vision focused, he saw that he was in a hospital room. Panicked, Andrew tried his best to move his arms and legs to get out of the bed. Feeling restrained, he tried his best to glance down, seeing his body was encased in a cast.

"What the hell did I do? What happened?" Andrew announced out loud, hoping something would provide him with answers.

Moments later, he heard the door open and some papers rustling.

"Mister Margruden, you took a nasty tumble. I'm pleased to see you're awake. Do you prefer Andrew?" the voice quizzed.

Andrew thought the voice was soothing and pleasant with a hint of authority. It must be the doctor.

"Yeah, Andrew is fine, doc."

"Great, great. I'll just be a moment with you," as the sound of rolling wheels filled the room, "and we can let you get some sleep."

Papers shuffled as Andrew grew more confused and panicked by the minute. The monitor he was attached to echoed his feelings.

"Now, Andrew, calm down. You're safe. You took quite a spill off the bridge in town a few weeks ago. Want to talk about what is going on?" the doctor asked, flipping through some pages of a file.

Andrew was puzzled. He wondered what bridge the doc was talking about, as well as how he ended up on the wrong side of it. The last thing he recalled was catching a rerun of Seinfeld late at night after the incident with his arm.

"As your doctor, I must ask if you feel you are planning to harm yourself in the future? We already had a previously documented incident."

Andrews's mind raced. *Hurt myself again? I didn't even hurt myself the first time.*

"Doc, what happened to me?" Andrew asked, afraid of what the answer might be.

The doctor scooted the stool closer to the bedside. He flipped through a few pages of the medical report before placing it on the table beside him.

"Quite frankly, Andrew, I don't know. To be frank, toxicology came back clean, and you have no history of mental illness. I'm stumped," the doctor explained. "It's part of the reason I've decided to just ask you for the missing puzzle piece in the hopes that you could complete the riddle."

Andrew sunk into himself. He couldn't figure out what was going on with him. All at once, it dawned on him: *the sleep drops.* They didn't detect any foreign medication in his bloodstream, though. Andrew felt that was a bit odd, making him not even want to bring it up.

"Get some rest, and we will revisit this conversation once you've slept," the doctor said as he closed the door on Andrew, leaving him to his thoughts.

Sleep. What is sleep? Andrew lay in bed, staring up at the ceiling for hours on end. Day after day, night after night, unable to sleep. The only release he would feel would be when his body would give out, unable to continue without shutting down from mental exhaustion. After spending time recovering at the hospital, he was released on his own cognition. Andrew now had an army of doctors to see going forward. Doctors that ranged from mental health to physical therapy. All he wanted to do was sleep.

Once back in the comfort of his own apartment, Andrew wheeled himself around as he tried to adjust back to a normal life. Perhaps the familiar smells, sounds, and environment would lull him into a peaceful sleep. As he sat listlessly in the wheelchair, a thought crossed back into his mind: *the drops.* He remembered the drops had a phone number for a doctor listed on the insert. With his lower body nearly unusable, he reached as best he could for the box containing the instructional leaflet. Balancing carefully to not tip his wheelchair, he gripped the corner of the box top, spilling the contents onto the table. The bottle of sleep aid rolled in his direction.

Andrew pondered for a moment. He considered precisely how much he could get into if he had another 'sleepwalking' episode. That's exactly what this was: sleepwalking. He had been deprived of uninterrupted sleep for so long, his body had no recollection of how to handle this newfound task. It made complete sense, at least, to Andrew. Using his good arm, he gripped the bottle and used his teeth to pry off the lid. It wasn't childproof in the least, thankfully. The dropper was easily accessible as well as fillable. He filled it with enough to take one drop.

"I'm not getting crazy. I know I'm chair-ridden, but for Christ's sake, look at all that's happened," he muttered out loud once again as he always did.

Squeezing one single drop on his tongue, he secured the bottle and returned it to the table. The paper with the instructions was sitting just outside of the box opening, which he reached for without hesitation. He read the instructions once again, this time, only more carefully. Side effects do not include waking up with broken bones or other injuries. He felt it best to reach out to the doctor for this one. Doctor Shatz. He had a good half hour until these things kicked in. Taking half a dose, likely he would have much longer. He dialed the number on his phone and waited through the gentle purr of the ring.

"Doctor Shatz's office. How can I help you?" a pleasant yet nasal-sounding voice greeted on the other end.

"Oh, um, uh," Andrew was caught off-guard. He didn't know what to expect, and it clearly wasn't this. "Doctor Shatz? I'm having issues with my medication and need to speak to Doctor Shatz."

"Hold, please."

The hold music was a simplified version of a song Andrew swore he knew but couldn't identify. He bobbed his head along, almost humming the tune before the line cracked and sprung to life.

"Doctor Shatz."

The voice was gruff, cold, and severe. No hint of bedside manner in this man's voice could be detected.

"Oh, Doc! I'm Andrew, and I had ordered your Sleep Aid."

"Mhmm?"

"I've been having some side effects that I think you should know about, is all," Andrew said, trying to push the conversation straight to the point.

"Side effects? Such as? Is it the explosive diarrhea? That one is prevalent in the patients," Doctor Shatz offered, assuming he knew the most common side effect was clearly the answer.

Andrew paused. How should he bring this up? What if it's not the meds, rather, himself? Perhaps it lies dormant for so long, triggered by a significantly deep sleep this medication provided?

"Well, it's complicated. I've been taking a few doses, and each time, well, hold on. Let me start by saying this stuff works like a charm. I've never fallen asleep so easily and slept so deeply." Andrew skirted around the problem by forming what he assumed should be the 'compliment sandwich.'

"I see."

"Well, Doc. You see, it's not that I don't think they're working, because they are. They work too well. So well, in fact, I believe I sleepwalk and end up hurting myself."

There was silence over the phone. Andrew was sure the doctor was judging him for such an unusual case of side effects. He closed his eyes for a moment in embarrassment and frustration. His eyes were a little heavier as he opened them.

"Okay. Let me clarify; Anthony, was it?"

"Andrew."

"Andrew. Andrew, let me be clear, and if I lose you, I apologize. Let me know, and I will clarify. Understood?" Doctor Shatz clearly articulated over the phone in a stern voice.

"Got it," Andrew groggily uttered.

"Andrew, what we are doing in my office is highly scientific, spiritual, and extremely experimental. Do you believe in the afterlife, Andrew?" Doctor Shatz calmly asked.

"I suppose. Do you mean when we cross over? Like heaven or hell? I guess so."

"Great. That is a good start. Well, we had been testing with the residual matter of the spirit world. Specifically, ectoplasmic traces and ionically charging them. My laboratory had nearly perfected a cure, if you will, for insomnia." Doctor Shatz seemed enthusiastic about the last part.

"Ok. You lost me, Doc," Andrew interrupted. His mind was aflutter with questions and clouded with a haze.

"Well, quite simply put, we used residue left behind by ghosts. Plain and simple, Andrew. You are experiencing a once-in-a-lifetime breakthrough! We can slip the subconscious of another individual, namely a spirit, into your body. In small doses, you slip away into dreamland while the spirit remains trapped in the host, er, body. Once processed, the spirit slips away and dissipates."

Andrew held the phone as close as he could to his ear as if what he heard didn't come through clearly. It was loud and clear: he was being dosed with ghosts.

"Now, Andrew, what side effects were you experiencing? Sleepwalking?" Doctor Shatz asked.

"Yes. I've woken up with broken body parts a few times. Most recently, I woke up from an incident in which I lept from a bridge. My femur is shattered, as is my pelvis and most of my spine. I survived, thank God," Andrew answered.

Silence filled the air. Andrew began to grow concerned that the doctor believed he was crazy.

"My dear Andrew, when did you last take the dosage? Have you disposed of the bottle?" the doctor asked, somewhat frantically.

"A bit before I called. But don't worry, it was only a half a dose."

"Egads! A half dose could still be fatal! It appears we had an anomaly in the system where the essence of a tormented spirit made its way into the safe batch. This is a quality control issue on a larger scale, I can assure you."

Andrew felt the phone slowly slipping away from his hands.

"Mr. Andrew. We will simply need your address, and we can have responders to your residence post haste. This is important, Andrew. What is your address?"

Silence filled the air on the other end of the line.

"Mr. Andrew! Hello? Are you still here? This could prove fatal if you take another dose. Andrew?" Doctor Shatz said frantically over the phone. His concern growing the more he called for Andrew.

Doctor Shatz held onto the line for a bit longer, only to hear a small amount of shuffling followed by a door opening in the background.

Andrew woke from his sleep. He couldn't hear anything over a deafening noise that whipped past his ears. Groggily, he opened his eyes, revealing the source of the sound. Below him, the hustle and bustle of the city. Above him, the night sky. Unfortunately for Andrew, nothing lying between either of them but himself for the next few moments. It was enough time, in his sluggish state, to deduce the rush of sound was that of the windows of the large building passing by he had most assuredly stepped off of moments ago. He only wished he had the bottle to take the rest of to sleep through this moment.

What really happened?

Well, none of this. Sorry. I never took magic ghost juice that made me jump off of things. However, I did and still have these strange sensations. Ever since I can recall, I've had them. They are more prevalent when I sleep face down, such as on a desk or table. I will frequently have the sensation I am falling.

In some cases, I'll visualize it too. It's terrifying. It always baffles me how a person can feel a sensation that they've never experienced before. How does my body know what it feels like to fall ten thousand feet? Perhaps I've done it back in a past life? I recall a few of the worst ones of my past.

Some of the milder ones involved me having the sensation of freefall, to be greeted by a loud screech of the desk as I jerked awake in grade school. After laugher died down, I'd go back to what I was doing. In other instances, I'd visualize a cliffside or building ledge that I'm falling from. I've had some of them where it's just a generic sky-filled freefall. Holy cow, those were the worst ones. I could feel my body tense up. I'd feel the wind against my body as it rushed past me. I could see the ground racing up to greet me. Complete body sensory overload to the point it felt real. I would always jerk wide awake every time before hitting the ground.

To this day, I still suffer from it. If I'm ever sleeping or on the cusp of it, I'll jerk awake violently; it's likely this very scenario. Equally, I suffer from insomnia and barely get rest. This could probably be a few factors that contribute to this ranging from **PTSD** to depression, etc. There once was a time I would have done almost anything to pass out asleep. I had tried them all; Ambien, Lunesta, etc. They only kept me awake and delusional. Nothing seemed to work for me. Hell, alcohol didn't do it for me either, and that can make anyone drowsy with the right amount. At this point, I've accepted it for what it is and use the awake time to write books, play video games, or build something. I just thought it would be fun to take something simple as insomnia and lucid dreams and make them terrifying. I apologize for the ending if you didn't like it, but I thought it would be interesting to have a form of possession as the reason this happens.

Father Figure

1

The winds whipped against the back window as the storm surge from hurricane Agnes whipped through the county. Outside, lawn furniture and other decorations took flight as if weightless, smashing into various structures or each other as they flew. When the wind was quieter, the torrential rains slapped against the roof like marbles on a hardwood floor. All of these sensations were terrifying for Paula and her children. She came to stay with her parents from the Midwest, only to be greeted by the storm of the century.

Harold, the eldest, tried his best to secure the property with his younger two brothers, Daniel and Richard. He did his best to keep calm and take care of their dear mother as she bailed buckets of water from the back kitchen door. Any drain system in place had failed, clogged with mud, and overflowing with rainwater. The children, more teenagers than children, pulled their weight to battle with the disaster scene found at their grandparents' home. While Harold helped bail water, Dan and Rich moved upstairs to ensure windows were not broken and the rain was not running into the house from other sources.

The following day, as quickly as it came, the storm had passed. Being so close to the Chesapeake Bay always posed a flood risk, but many disregarded the warnings. An exhausted Paula peered from the kitchen window that overlooked the bay. The view had always been a beautiful one. The sunrise would gently peek over the trees on the horizon, and the waves would lap against the shore just ahead. Today, the coast was the back door. The sunrise was masked by the thick dark clouds of the storm and nearby structure fires.

The rebuilding began. The family home stood, as it always had in the past. This structure weathered countless storms and at least three wars. Harold went outside with his younger brothers and began collecting sticks, debris, and trash from the property. Paula stayed inside and did her best to clean up what she could.

"Paula, let me help you with that, dear," a voice said from down the hallway.

Paula's father, Samuel, stood tall and proud at the end of the hall. His stature was that of a professional strongman from the heyday of the circus. As strong as he looked, he never let on that he was dying from stage four cancer.

"Father, I can take care of it. You rest. You're not well," Paula said, trying her best to usher her father back into the bedroom verbally. "You have a doctor's appointment, and I'll have to phone the office to see if they're open today. Rest up."

"Oh, I'll rest when I'm dead, dear. Let me help you with this. I'm not an involent," Samuel replied acrimoniously.

Paula gave up the fight and allowed her father to help sop up some of the water. He even took a few buckets of water to the bathroom to drain. Paula was afraid he really would rest when he was dead with the way he worked. Sam was a former Navy sailor, retired police officer, and local neighborhood watchman. This man didn't know the definition of quit; he was a fighter. He swore if cancer were something he could punch in the jaw, he would have knocked its lights out long ago.

Edna, Paula's mother, emerged from the bedroom soon after the last bucket of water was dumped.

"Samuel! You put that bucket down right this instant and relax!" Edna exclaimed.

Sam immediately set the bucket on the floor and stepped away with his hands up towards his chest.

"Now, you get downstairs and rest in your easy chair until we need to get you to your appointment," Edna continued to scold.

Sam responded with some murmurs under his breath but ultimately complied. Compliance and complaint, this was Samuel's typical form. Slowly and painfully, he shifted himself toward his easy chair. He eased himself down gently as his family went back to their hustle and bustle of the morning. He watched the world flutter as his children helped Edna pack belongings for the extended stay at the hospital ahead of them. A typical visit usually called for an overnight stay, if not the entire weekend.

"Good news, Pop! The doctor is still open, and the storm barely touched the hospital. By the grace of God, they managed to come out unscathed," said Rich.

"Oh, my word. It's your lucky Day, Samuel!" Edna exclaimed as she put her hat and coat on.

The weather was settled to a mild drizzle of rain as the three boys watched Edna escort their ill father to the car. After a few moments of idling in the driveway, they drove off over the horizon.

"You think Pop will be fine?" Harold asked his younger siblings, trying not to sound too alarmed.

Dan rubbed his chin in deep thought. "Pop is strong; he'll pull through."

As Dan finished his sentence, a vase kept on an old wooden table crashed to the floor in the upstairs hallway.

"The heck was that?" Harold asked as he displayed signs of concern.

Rich shrugged. "Let's check it out?"

The three brothers ventured together toward the wreckage of the vase. The table was standing, and nothing out of the ordinary at play. It was a wide-based vase, so the chances of it toppling over were slim.

"Huh. The house musta settled, and it fell," said Harold, trying to reassure his brothers that it was ok.

Richard was staring down the hallway intently at something. The other brothers noticed.

"What is it, Dick?" Dan asked his brother, adjusting his gaze to match Richard's.

Once his brothers met his stare, Richard shook his head in disbelief.

"I saw... Nevermind."

"What did you see?" asked Harold.

"It sounds stupid. I saw a shadow down the hall. It turned and headed toward mom and dad's room."

Rich seemed visibly shaken. There was no reason for his brothers not to believe him.

The three non-verbally agreed that heading downstairs and sticking together in the sitting room after cleaning the vase would be best. The boys played their favorite board game to pass the time. Always looking over their shoulders, the boys felt the hours they waited were like years as Edna, Paula, and Sam returned from the hospital. Sam made his way straight to the bedroom with the aid of Paula. Edna joined the boys.

"Playing a fun game, are we?" Edna asked.

Richard shrugged. "Yeah. It's better than the monster we saw."

Edna's expression changed. "Monster, you say?"

Dan punched Richard hard in the arm. "Shut up, Dick, or I'll pound you again. We didn't see nothin'."

Edna sat forward in her rocking chair. Her expression seemed to be one not of surprise but understanding.

"So, you boys have seen him too?"

"Yeah," the three said in unison.

"Oh my, oh my. This isn't good. I was afraid this day would come," Edna said with palpable trouble in her tone.

"What, Grandma? What's going on?" Harold asked.

"I'm going to assume you boys saw the Shadow Man?" Edna asked casually.

The expressions on the faces of each of the three boys spoke louder than words. Each of them shot a glance at the other.

"I remember back when I was younger, and your grandfather would step away on business. What a time that was. He was constantly traveling. This was the first time I saw the Shadow Man, you see."

"Well, Grandma, what happened?" Dan asked eagerly.

Edna glanced toward the staircase to see if her daughter was in earshot. After deciding the coast was clear, she began to tell the tale. The boys set down their cards and gave their full attention.

"Well, it was one day long ago. Sam, rather, your grandfather, was due to travel to Pittsburg for a sales conference of sorts," Edna began. "We hadn't been in this house more than a few weeks before business picked up."

"Oh, the house was new, Grandma?" Richard asked.

"Oh, heavens, no. This house had been around much longer than any of us under this roof. At the time, it was a new house for us. We were happy to be in it."

"So, what happened?" Harold questioned.

Edna looked at Harold. "Patience is a virtue. I'm getting there. When your grandfather went off for his trip, I was terrified of being alone in this house. Everything creaked that could creak. The moans moaned. At first, I assumed I had imagined it."

The boys shifted a bit in their seats, displaying feelings of unease.

"I had just stepped out of the bathroom after getting ready for the day. Down the hall, a man stood. Only, it wasn't a man," Edna corrected herself, "it was more of a shadow."

"That's what we saw!" Dan exclaimed as the other two boys agreed.

"For years, I begged Samuel to stay home. I was terrified of being alone. He told me to stop being silly and find a hobby. That was when I began working at the library to get out of the house. The less I had to be here, the better."

"Oh, you worked at the library?" Harold asked.

"Yes, a long time ago. Now back to my story. I only noticed the shadow when I was alone. Whenever your grandfather was at work, I was afraid for my very life. When he was home, it seemed to be afraid of him."

"Is that why we saw it, Grandma?" asked Richard.

"I believe that is exactly why, Richard."

The boys shot each other a look of horror. Being trapped in this house due to the storm made it hard for them to get back to their own home with their mother, Paula. The roads didn't sound like they were too bad, but was their mother willing to leave her father in such a state?

Paula rounded the corner. "What are you talking about?"

"Oh, we were just discussing the board game. How is Samuel? Should I go check on him, and you stay with the boys?"

"Sure. I'll sit with them. Dad's not doing too well."

Edna frowned a bit before starting around the corner up the stairs. Her feet shuffled slowly on the wooden staircase, which creaked every so often.

2

The days were seeming darker for the family. Samuel, in his many years of strength fighting his illness, lost his battle with cancer. Try as they might, the doctors were unable to do anything for him. That was the story Edna and Paula told the boys. The reality of the situation was that Sam had been on a gradual slope to the inevitable for several years. The fact that he held on for nearly a decade astonished his care physicians.

In the days that Sam spent at the hospital, the boys hung out between their home and their grandmother's. They made the best of it, trying to have friends over to ease the loneliness of the rest of the family attending to hospital matters and eventual funeral proceedings. Billy, one of Danny's long-time friends, offered to stay the night with the guys. The plan was to sneak off to the local theater and watch a movie, followed by a quick bite to eat at Anne's Dari Creme for a footlong hotdog. It was the local eatery hangout where all the cool kids went.

Following the movie, the boys went to Anne's as planned.

"So, Billy, can we tell you something?" asked Dan.

"Sure, Dan. What's up?"

"So, this is going to sound ridiculous, but we think our grandmother's house is haunted."

Harold and Richard nodded their heads in agreement.

"Haunted, you say?" Bill asked as he took a large bite from his footlong. "Well-f, Mffif youf branted to bo a broskhurnt."

"English, Bill. Finish your food," Harold said as he took a sip from his strawberry milkshake.

Bill swallowed, cleaning the ketchup from his cheek and the chili from his nose. "Oh, I was going to say if you wanted to do a ghost hunt, I should get my camera! My pop has a nice one, and it spits the photo out right away."

"Oh, good idea! Meet at my grandma's place at ten?" Dan asked.

"You got it, brother," Bill responded as he shoved the rest of the footlong chili hotdog into his face.

A few hours went by, and the boys were wondering where Bill went off to. It was a quarter after ten, and they were growing concerned. Harold threw a few logs into the fire in the den as they played more Monopoly.

"You think Bill is ok?" Harold asked as he dusted his hands off from the wood.

"Oh, sure. He's likely —" Dan started as he was interrupted by a loud, obnoxious rapping at the front door.

Rich got up to open the door for Bill.

"Oh, I got some stuff for tonight, too! This should be fun. It's in the trunk; give me a hand?" Bill said as he started off the porch down to his Buick.

The boys were astonished to find that Bill not only brought his camera but a few bottles of beer and a bottle of vodka. In addition to the drinks, a handful of snacks.

"Gee, where did you get this beer and stuff, Bill?" asked Harold.

"My Pa, but he won't mind. He's got plenty. Now let's have a good night and find us a ghost!"

The night went on as Bill, Harold, Dan, and Rich drank beverages they shouldn't, ate food they should avoid, and shared stories of an inappropriate nature. A thud came from upstairs, interrupting the latest tale of women and manly adventures from Bill and Dan.

"What the heck was that?" asked Bill.

"That's probably him," said Harold.

"Him?" asked Bill.

"Him. The Shadow Man," answered Dan.

The boys cleaned up their immediate surroundings and secured the camera. Bill checked the lens and ensured it had power.

"It's ready to rock and roll if you guys are," Bill said as he motioned to investigate the source of the noise.

The four of them slowly made their way from the den to the main hallway. The stairway seemed darker than ever before. Every bit of light seemed to snuff out along the way. Harold flicked the light switch that went to the upstairs hall. A sickly orange glow flooded the hallway as they ascended the staircase.

"You think we'll see it?" asked Dan.

"Shhh," said Harold, "of course we'll see it. If we don't, that means we're crazy, and we're not crazy."

"I think you both are crazier than squirrel turds, to be honest," Bill said jokingly.

"It's nuttier, Bill," Harold scoffed.

"You've tasted?" laughed Bill.

Harold scowled and returned his gaze to the foreboding hall. The quartet of teenagers made their way down the hallway, panning from side to side. Every shadow appeared to be a threat. Each dark corner posed a safety concern. The Shadow Man lurked in just about every nook and cranny the boys couldn't see.

"There isn't a damn thing up here, guys," Bill started, "I brought my dad's camera for nuthin'."

Richard had stopped walking. He stood still, silently staring down the opposite end of the hallway.

"What's your problem, Dick?" Dan asked his brother while trying to look past him. "Shit! Bill, get the camera!"

Bill moved as fast as his feet would allow. He whirled around with the Polaroid and snapped a shot. The photo ejected out of the front with a deafening grinding noise. No one had noticed how quiet it had been until the silence was interrupted by machinery.

"Well, did ya see it?" asked Dan.

"No. I don't know. I mean, I didn't see anything. You said shoot, so I shooted. What else you want from me, guys?" Bill said as he waved the photograph in the air to develop it.

The boys looked around for the Shadow Man. Everything upstairs seemed eerily normal to them.

"Take the photo downstairs and finish the party? Let's listen to some tunes on the player," Bill said as he started down the stairs, still flicking the photograph in his hands.

The foursome sat around the coffee table in the den once more. The room was a disaster, full of empty bags of snacks and a few bottles of alcohol. Harold tried to be the responsible one and began cleaning it up.

"I'll grab you a trash can, Har," Dan said as he moved toward the kitchen.

As Dan passed the threshold of the room, a noise on his right nearly caused him to jump out of his skin.

Ring.......ring......ring....

The telephone nearly caused Dan to have a heart attack right there in front of everyone.

"Answer it, Dan!" commanded Richard.

Dan hesitantly picked up the receiver.

"H—Hello?" He stammered.

"Hey, who's this?" a female voice asked on the other end.

"You called us! Who's this?" responded Dan.

The voice giggled for a moment. "It's Katie. Is this Danny?"

Dan shook his head yes before verbally responding with a yes. His heart rate was still working to return to normal. "Hey guys, it's Katie!" he called to the group. Richard rushed over.

The two boys shared the receiver to talk to Katie. Richard was great friends with her but always wanted something more. Dan also had an infatuation with her. The boys shared the phone to listen in.

"So, I was thinking. Maybe we could go out next weekend? Just the two of us, Rich?" Katie asked, knowing Daniel was still on the phone.

"Sure! That sounds swell, honestly. I need to get out and do something fun," Richard replied, a slight smile and blush forming on his face.

As Richard and Dan listened on Katie's weekend plans, something caught Dan's eye. A faint movement to his left sent his heart racing. He let go of the receiver of the phone to get a better look.

"R—Rich. Rich, look!" Dan yelled out as his finger burst through the air to point.

Richard turned his attention to the target of Dan's pointing. For a split second, he saw it. The Shadow Man had faded out of view at the foot of the stairs. He was standing as if he had been watching the group the whole time. Richard and Daniel unanimously dropped the receiver to the table, which bounced to dangle toward the floor. They screamed as loudly as they could, alerting the other two before bursting through the front door.

Harold and Bill didn't waste time with questions. Bill grabbed his camera and photograph and headed toward the door with Harold. The door slammed behind them as they rushed toward Bill's car. No one ever determined if they shut the door behind them or if something unnatural closed it for them. The car sped off to a nearby gas station.

Under the lights of the gas station, the group caught a breather.

"Well, did that photo develop?" asked Dan.

"Oh, hell, I almost forgot!" Bill said, reaching into his vest pocket.

He withdrew the photo from his jacket and took a hard look at it before anyone else could. Before he knew it, six sets of eyes were transfixed on the picture, trying to discern what they were seeing.

"Damnit! I moved too fast with the camera!" Bill said as he tossed the photograph onto the dashboard.

Dan took another look at the photo. It was true; the only evidence they had was a blurry shot. A shot that nothing conclusive would ever come from. They left empty-handed.

3

Paula returned home from the funeral. The boys went off to mourn and be together. She barely scolded them about the drinking, given the circumstances of everything. Between the storm and deaths in the family, she understood. She was thankful they at least decided to stay in the house and party rather than drive around and hurt someone or themselves.

She had cleaned up the disaster without question. The death of Samuel had numbed her mentally and spiritually. She found it was nice to focus on something outside of his departure for a change. The funeral was emotionally and physically taxing. The boys were handling it in their way, so who was she to scold them?

Days went by as Edna was visited daily by her daughter, Paula. Paula felt guilty for leaving her to return home for work. However, there was no other alternative. The bills still needed to be paid. Each day, she would ask the same series of questions of Edna.

"Ma, do you need anything?" Paula asked.

"No, dear. I told you I'm fine. I'll manage," Edna would reply without haste.

"Are you sure I can't get you anything?" Paula pestered.

"I assure you I will get on just fine," Edna said.

This mood went on for the first three or four days. Paula was asking Edna partly due to the fact she was trying to find a way to cope. Losing her father took a lot out of her, and she hated to admit it.

Paula returned to the house in the late afternoon, as she always had. She knew Edna stepped away for a late lunch with a friend from the senior center but tended to the house regardless.

The front door creaked open eerily. The very sound sent waves of sensations down Paula's spine. Something about the way it sounded bothered her today. She pressed on, turning on the lights in the main rooms. She made her way to the kitchen and began tending to the dishes. Edna wasn't unable to take care of things, but Paula didn't want her mother to worry about a thing. Even if it meant her time was sacrificed.

After completing a clean-up of the kitchen, Paula moved to check the bedrooms and make any beds as necessary. The guest room was typically never an issue, so she walked straight for Edna's room. The staircase creaked and moaned under her every step. Once at the top of the stairs, she flipped on the hallway light. The sickly orange-like glow of the lamps filled the area.

Down the hallway, the shadows played tricks on Paula. She paid no mind to them and entered Edna's bedroom. She reached out for the light string housed under the side table lamp and tugged it. With a click, it illuminated the room. The bed had been made. The laundry was in order. There was barely a thing to fix in the place. Stricken without a purpose, she sank into the bed and began to sob. The reality of everything hitting her with another wave once again.

Paula wiped the tears from her eyes upon hearing a strange noise from the hallway. She assumed Edna returned home from her luncheon and casually made her way out of the bedroom. There, in the now pale-lit hallway, stood a figure in the darkness of the corner. Paula rubbed her eyes a bit, assuming that the tears she had been crying had caused irritation or obstruction. The figure was still there and only moved closer.

"I'm leaving!" Paula screamed out as she darted for the staircase.

She felt a push on the small of her back, causing her to lose her footing, stumbling down the staircase. Tumbling four or five stairs, Paula regained control and returned to leaving on foot. She left all of the lights on and only managed to grab her purse on the way out. In her haste, Paula left her jacket behind on her father's easy chair. She slammed the door on the way out. Paula found herself waiting at the end of the street in her car for her mother to return home.

Once Edna returned, only an hour later from the incident, Paula insisted that she not enter the house. She pleaded to her mother to stay with her and the boys tonight until the next day.

"Can I at least get my belongings?" Edna asked her panicked daughter.

"I'll go with you. I don't want to go back in there, but I also don't want you in there alone with that thing," Paula replied to her mother.

Edna frowned. "The Shadow Man? He hasn't bothered me at all. I've seen him pass by now and again with no harm coming to me."

"Ma. He, or it, shoved me down the stairs today. I don't trust the house. Can we get what you need and get out?"

Enda started toward the house. Her body language said it all. She wasn't afraid of this entity, shadow, or whatever it was that was scaring the daylights out of her family. Paula followed close behind as Edna unlocked and opened the door to the home. The air was thick, and the feeling was heavy inside. Something was very off.

As the two navigated toward the bedroom to pack an overnight bag, the air practically began to choke them. It was as if someone or something had removed the oxygen from the room. Their bodies felt more lethargic the longer they remained in the home. Finally, Edna was packed.

Paula helped her mother carry the two bags of belongings down the stairs. Once at the bottom of the staircase, she spotted something moving to her right. She assumed it could only be one thing: the Shadow Man. Paula took her mother by the arm and pulled her onward toward the door. Whatever compelled her to glance over at the moving object, she will never know.

To her right, she saw the Shadow Man standing near her late father's easy chair. It was almost clutching it as an act of triumph or defiance. She didn't have time to find out more.

"We have to go, Ma!" Edna called to her mother as she thrust open the door.

The Shadow Man crept closer toward the two women as they stepped through the threshold, slamming the door behind them and hurrying to the car. Paula fumbled with the keys for a moment, threw the car into drive, and sped home with no intention to look back at the home until it was daylight.

The next day, the funeral home called and advised Paula that her father's ashes were available to pick up.

"I can bring the ashes myself after my shift ends if it will help make things easier for you, Paula," the director offered. There was genuine kindness in his tone.

Paula hesitated. Just yesterday, they were fleeing the home. Perhaps if the director is in the house with them, she can stall him while her mother grabs more prized belongings.

"That works. What time will you be by?" Paula asked.

"After five. I'll close up the shop and can be there soon after. I do not have any clients on the books today," the director responded.

The hours passed like seconds. The dread of stepping foot into the home nearly drove Paula to insanity. The boys hadn't returned home from school and were likely playing with Billy. She preferred they be together and away from this situation.

"Ma, we're going back to the house to pick up a few things and meet with the funeral director. He's been so kind as to deliver father to us himself," Paula shouted to the bedroom of the hotel to Edna.

"Great, dear. I'll get my coat and be ready in a jiffy."

The two women traveled to Edna's home. Neither wanted to be in the house, particularly Paula. With the events that unfolded, she wanted no part of that building or the Shadow Man. The drive over took no time at all. Every effort Paula took to drag the time out or procrastinate was futile. Each light was green. Cars moved when they were supposed to. Not one single detour or diversion to delay the process. They pulled up in front of Edna's home in record time. The funeral director's car was parked just out front.

"I hope you weren't waiting too long?" Edna asked the man as she stepped up to him in front of his vehicle.

"Oh, not at all. It's the least I can do. How are you doing, my dear?" the director said as he offered a hug to the widow.

"I've been better. It doesn't feel real, but we both accepted that we'd lived a long and full life. We had a happy marriage. We produced wonderful children and grandchildren. What more can someone ask for?" replied Edna.

"That's true. Now, to the matter at hand," the director said, presenting a small cardboard box. "Let's head inside, shall we?"

The trio moved their way to the porch, entering the home. The director followed closely as the women made their way into the den.

"He always loved this room the most," Edna said.

"Indeed. I bet Sam did. A fine room, equipped with a fireplace and this lovely easy chair to relax by it in."

The director pulled the urn from the cardboard and placed it on the mantle of the fireplace. Almost immediately, Paula felt the haze over the house lift. The air became clear and crisp as a fresh spring morning.

"If you need anything from us at all, do not hesitate to ask, my dear. We can set you up with the finest grief counselors," the director turned to Paula. "That goes for you too, dear."

With a smile, he turned and showed himself out of the home.

"What a nice gentleman," Edna said to her daughter as she began to straighten the den up a bit.

"Ma, I'll grab some things from the bathroom. Anything else you need?" Paula asked.

"No, dear. I'll be fine for a few more days until you stop worrying about this house."

Paula thought to herself that she would never stop worrying. Her father seemed always to keep that monster at bay, and with him gone, it was free to run amok. She slowly made her way up the staircase. The very same stairs that she tumbled down not one day ago.

As she rounded the turn, Paula flipped on the hallway light. The same sickening glow flooded the area once more. Once at the top of the stairs, she looked down the hallway. There was no shadow or looming figure to be seen. Now was her chance to act quickly. Maybe the Shadow Man was sleeping.

She moved into the bathroom, grabbing toothbrushes and soaps. She tossed those into a generic shopping bag she brought from the car before moving out toward the bedroom.

Before she could get across the hallway, a familiar feeling crept over her body. She felt as if someone was looking at her. Slowly, Paula looked back down the hall toward the slightly shadow-filled end. There, in the corner, stood a humanoid figure. The Shadow Man, as she had seen before. It started toward her immediately. Quickly, Paula panicked and darted into her mother's bedroom. The Shadow Man was fast behind.

As Paula stumbled over the bed, she assumed this was the end.

"Please! Please! No, leave me alone! Leave me alone!" Paula felt her body tremble with trepidation.

The Shadow Man crept across the room slowly. It seemed to enjoy the fear and torment. Paula backed up toward the wall opposite the door. Slowly, she closed her eyes for what would seem like the last time.

A bright light flashed out across the room. Paula squinted as she opened her eyes slightly to see a second figure in the room. The Shadow Man appeared to cower and dissipated in front of her. The power and intensity of the blinding light never faltered. The glow from the illumination felt warm and safe. She tried to look through the slits of her fingers as she covered her face with her hand. The radiant figure seemed to be that of her father.

As the light began to fade and the illuminated figure started to disappear, she could clearly see that it was, in fact, Samuel. He was healthy-looking and smiling as strong as ever. He gave her a wink as he disappeared. Paula dropped the bag of toiletries she had been gripping for dear life.

Slowly, Paula made her way downstairs to join Edna. She found her sitting next to the easy chair with a roaring fire in the fireplace.

"Ma, we have to leave, remember?" asked Paula.

Edna turned and looked at her. A calm look washed over her face.

"I take it you saw your father?" she asked.

Paula was startled. How could she know? Surely she could have heard the screaming, but this?

"Don't worry. I know all about it. Samuel stopped by and asked me to light this fire and wait. He was going to go see to it that the Shadow Man never bothered me again," Edna started to say.

"Wait, father was here?" Paula interrupted.

"Yes, he came to me. He sat in his chair and asked that I light his fire the way he liked. He told me to sit down beside him and wait for him as he took care of a few chores around the house. I could only assume he meant the Shadow Man."

Paula sat on a small stool that rested in front of her father's easy chair.

"Wait, you mean father knew about the Shadow Man, too?" asked Paula.

"Of course he did. He never doubted me for a minute. The fact that it never hurt me was likely because something about Samuel terrified it. That thing had been here for years! Even as you grew up," Edna said with a smile.

The thought of growing up with the Shadow Man in the home all of her life troubled Paula deeply. She'd never seen it because her father was always home. Once she moved away, she likely never noticed anything out of the ordinary because she would visit when he was back from business trips or holidays.

The whole thing clicked for Paula. Her father had always been the protector of the family. His ashes being returned brought him back to fulfill his duties as protector of the household. Now that he was able to do battle with the evil spirit on its terms, he succeeded. She only hoped that her father would return to check on her mother every so often as she began to restore the packed items to the proper locations.

What was the inspiration?

This one was a cool one to put on paper, but I can't take credit for the idea. As I always try to do with my stories, I share some personal experiences that terrified the crap out of me and fictionalized it. I know you're wondering where in the world this one came from. I've already had accusations on the Internet about "stealing" stories, even though these are things I've experienced. Well, I'm coming clean on this one; I never experienced this story. My grandmother, father, uncles, and a few other individuals did.

My grandparents are full of the greatest stories, as most grandparents are. Being around as long as they have, grandparents are likely to have, quite literally, seen and done it all. They've been there and done that long before you were considered. Particularly when it comes to life experiences, they've been around the block with those. When it comes to death experiences, I can assure you, they also have you beat. Heck, I've lost many friends to war, suicide, or natural causes at my age. Could you imagine decades and decades of existence?

They've sat down and shared stories about hauntings in their bedroom where relatives have visited. They've shared stories that I'll likely reserve for future books because they're so exciting. My grandfather has one in particular about a mass witnessing of a woman walking into the kitchen and sitting down at the table, taking her ears off as if they were jewelry. More on that in future books, but as I said, they've seen some things in their life.

 This story, in particular, stems from a dark entity that resided in my grandmother's old home in Severna Park, MD, no more than a quick stroll from where I grew up. I don't recall ever being in this house myself. Likely it was before my time. Not being there myself, I thought it would be fun to take a story that was told to me a few times and turn it into my own.

 My dad and uncles were teenagers when the actual events took place. My grandparents were probably in their early forties or late thirties if I had to take a wild shot at it. They all have their own experiences and stories that build on the overall story that shares similarities to the tale I told before. They all centered around the same shadow figure that haunted the home. Each of the experiences I shared mainly were versions of the stories they each told me. They all ended up with the same result: when grandfather was home, that spirit wanted nothing to do with him. That much was apparent.

Roulette

Bonus Short Short Story

Two men are sitting around a wooden table. The fire roars and crackles behind them from the fireplace. The cabin they are lodging in is drafty but not unpleasant. It is located just a few miles from a nearby lake, isolated from civilization. On the table is a bottle of fine bourbon, fifty years aged. Placed directly adjacent are two highball glasses, half full of the dark liquor. The men look at each other, exhausted and bored.

"You wan play again, Clyde?" the first man asked, his rough backwoods accent apparent.

Clyde takes a sip from his glass and rubs his chin in deep thought.

"Christ, Clyde, I ain't got all dang day. It's your turn if you wan go."

Clyde looked at his companion. He wasn't sure how to proceed. There was a lot of hesitation in his voice as he spoke.

"Wilbur, you take the honors this time. I'm tired of going first. You feelin' lucky?" Clyde finally croaked out.

Wilbur looked at the Ruger Single-Six placed neatly in the center of the table. He pondered and thought for a moment before reaching for the handgun. Cocking back the hammer, Wilbur put the end of the cold steel barrel against his temple. He made eye contact with Clyde.

"Want me to count ya down, Wilbur?" Clyde asked eagerly as his comrade placed the barrel of the revolver to his head.

Wilbur smiled. "Sure, go ahead. Do the honors, if it please."

Clyde took a hard sip from his glass before counting. He knew the moments before squeezing that trigger were the tensest moments in anyone's life. The wind began to pick up once more outside as the silence was broken by the howl of a crisp draft through the front door.

"One," Clyde began.

Wilbur was shaking a bit but steeled himself for the following number.

"Two," Clyde said with a smile. He leaned forward a bit into the table before finishing the next number.

"Oh, God dangit out with it, will ya!" Wilbur shouted as he lowered the revolver to yell.

Clyde looked upset. "Don't you go yellin' at me if'n you ain't tryin' to pull that trigger now, Wilbur."

The shutters on the outside window began to slap against the frame of the window. The restraints were holding but had worn with age. The banging sound was coupled with the intense howl of the late evening wind.

"You gon' do it or what, Wil?" Clyde asked once more.

"I'll do it, dangit. Say three."

Clyde rested back in his chair, placing a boot up on the table. He took one long sip to finish the rest of his Bourbon from his glass, licking his lips before speaking.

"Three."

Wilbur pressed the barrel hard against his temple and began to squeeze the trigger. The hammerlock went back ever slightly, and the barrel rotated to the next chamber.

*Click.

Wilbur let out a sigh of relief as he dropped the handgun back onto the table.

"You sumbitch, I thought that was it. Your turn, Clyde!" Wilbur said with a laugh.

Clyde reached for the revolver and flicked the barrel to spin to a new location. He pressed it to his temple, as Wilbur did before him.

"Want me to count you in, Clyde?" Wilbur asked as he crossed his arms and smiled.

"I'll do it myself, feller. Thanks," Clyde responded.

The fire rippled and crackled as the draft came down the fireplace chimney. One of the shutters worked itself loose and was now slapping against the side of the window hard. Clyde took a few deep breaths before moving his finger to the trigger. He slowly squeezed his index finger, feeling the mechanical parts of the handgun moving into action.

*BANG

The gun fired off, and Clyde slumped onto the table. There was an odd silence that filled the air.

"Goddangit, Clyde! You are terrible at this game! This is the fourth time you done lost tonight. Can we play something else?" Wilbur asked, standing up from the table.

Clyde sat up after a few moments. He shook his head dramatically and put the pistol back into his holster.

"I got poker if you're a gamblin' man," Clyde said as he poured himself a new drink.

What the heck was that?

Roulette was a short-short story that I submitted for a short story contest with the Veterans Affairs creativity office. I obviously didn't experience this one in the least but felt it more than decent enough to share with the rest of the world. This one actually came together quickly once the idea hit me.

I had been lying in bed when it hit me. Much like most of my book ideas, such as FUBAR, I needed to quickly jot something down. I jammed into my phone something to the effect of "Two guys playing Russian roulette. One guy loses. The other guy says, 'you suck at this game, let's play Monopoly.'" It's incredible how something so quick and brief can spawn off something that becomes "Roulette."

I submitted this story along to the VA, assuming it would end up in the junk pile of submissions. Surprisingly, it was accepted, thankfully, and I was on my way to the state finals! I took a day to drive almost an hour from my home to the hosting VA center, only to see nine other submissions on the table next to mine! I was pretty freaked out.

I wandered around, looking at the fine art, photographs, and models decorated around the room.

There was so much talent. I decided to take a read at the 'competition.' There were submissions named "SWAG," "Phoenix," and "The Note," among so many others. I thumbed through each entry. I never let anyone know my submission was on the table. "The Note" was well written, and a sad story that I felt was top tier.

People were reading the stories as they passed by the table. One by one, they'd either close the document early or show an expression of happiness or grief depending on the story. The reactions were all the same, except for Roulette. Every single time someone picked it up, their demeanor changed. It went from a basic, "Hmm, what ever could this be?" to a full-blown, "What the hell am I reading?" followed by a slight smirk as they set the book down. Well? Did they like it?

You bet they did. Every person I asked what they thought about it said it was a fun little read. They pictured everything from some old Civil War soldiers to the brothers from Supernatural. What a contrast, right? The general public seemed to enjoy it, which was nice. The judges already reviewed and graded the works but failed to post the scores or winner ribbons. We inquired, and they began to rate everything.

Each category was given a first, second, and third place, respectively. They started with the bronze third place winners. Poems were rated separately from short stories, so I had a fighting chance. I was still up against "The Note" and other quality writings. They placed a bronze marker on a few works. "Roulette" remained untouched. I assumed if I didn't make third, I wasn't making it at all.

The judges then stuck silver stickers onto the second-place winners. One of the entrants was miscategorized, and they recategorized as a short-short story. This put some fear into me. I hadn't been judged yet, but I wasn't winning. This woman received the silver sticker for second-place. Honestly, I don't know that she'd have done as well with the poetry category. Kudos to her.

Then came the gold. "The Note" grabbed the gold for inspirational short story, a whole different category from the short-short story where "Roulette" was placed. It deserved that rank. Heck, everyone wrote good stuff that day. I saw a gold sticker get plastered right on the front of my paper. First place Short-Short story. What?!

By the time this book comes out, the story will have already advanced to the Nationals. I felt it was a unique, fun, and entertaining little read that fit best in this collection of stories. I only hope it was as fun to read this story as it was to write.

The Frozen Eye

From the "Once Upon a Dystopia" anthology

Once upon a time, in a land far away, the kingdom of Windvale had been cast into darkness. A once-prosperous settlement, Windvale had come upon the curse of a powerful witch. This witch, you see, had a dark curse upon her. Her curse, which none of the townsfolk could understand, was the power to manipulate water and ice. For this power, you see, came at a price. The Queen had to be locked away atop a frozen mountainside, with her palace resting upon a perpetually frozen lake. If she left her fortress, she would soon feel the heat of the sun upon her flesh, causing her to melt.

For ages, The Queen stayed in her castle, overseeing the kingdom. Windvale was unaffected by her rule at first, allowing her to attain more and more power. Before the kingdom knew what had happened, she had seized the ruling class's power, killing them within her frigid fortress. The townsfolk knew this did not bode well. Reality set in further as the ice crept further from her frozen moat, down the green grassy mountainside, into the bustling town square. The fountain froze in place. Windows shattered. Those that were unwise found themselves trapped in a thick layer of ice. The ones that were smart enough to stay indoors, such as young Alma and her parents, found themselves spared from the frigid death that encroached upon the land.

Years had passed in the kingdom of Windvale. People learned to work around the ice sheets but were generally displeased by the situation they found themselves in. Now practically an adult, Alma began to wonder exactly what she could do to spend her day. She had completed her chores in the home. Ever since her mother passed from a terrible fever, she picked up the household tasks, helping her father as often as she could. Her father was once a fit and robust lumberjack. He would fell any tree with his bare hands and a trusty ax. Now, when Alma looked upon him, he could barely get out of bed. A terrible sickness and sadness had come upon Windvale.

Alma stepped outside of her home, gazing up at the grey overcast sky. Every day was bleak and drab. The mood was reflected on her various neighbors' faces as they moped along, trying to complete daily chores.

"This is absolute madness!" Alma yelled out to nobody in particular. "I recall the sun, the grass, the rolling hills."

Alma did remember. As a child, she remembered playing with the neighbor child, Ella, in a vast field of daisies and other beautiful flowers. A fleeting memory, but vivid nonetheless. A blast of cold air snapped Alma out of her daydreams and fantasies. She was greeted once again by the cold, uninviting wasteland that was once her beautiful home. Another blast of cold air snapped at her cheek. She turned to see the Ice Queen, hovering gently above the ground, encased in a whirlwind of snow. She floated toward the town square, which Alma crept around to view.

"People of Windvale! It has come to my attention that I, your beautiful, wonderful Queen, have failed you in a way," The Queen announced, her voice coming through clear over the howl of the winds.

Townsfolk began to gravitate toward the town square. Most never saw the Queen or her power. They heard stories, and that was enough for them. Here she stood, addressing the nation she reigned over.

"I come to you, my people, urging you to cheer up! Have I not given you protection from enemy ships? Invading armies? Barbarians who would surely do unspeakable things to your women and children?" The Queen boomed across the town.

There was a moment of discussion amongst the townsfolk before their queen raised her hand once more to stifle the crowd. The sound instantly went away.

"People of windvale! I fear that it is your mood that brings this town and its morale down."

One man stepped forward. "Our mood? My Queen, are you insane? Take a look around! It's miserable here! Everything is grey and white; we 'avent seen the sun in ages, m'lady. Pardon my speech, but this is why morale is low."

The Queen floated toward the ground, seating herself on the edge of the fountain. She seemed to be in deep thought as the townsfolk looked at each other with confused expressions. Muttering amongst the town began to drum up once more before The Queen raised her hand again to silence them.

"I have a solution to our situation. It appears you are not happy, and I can recognize that. You live in a beautiful part of the land, adorned with the finest and purest of snow," The Queen bellowed. "You should smile more. Believing in this kingdom as I do will help you feel pleasure and love as I do!"

The townsfolk once again muttered amongst themselves while Alma watched on. She was curious about what was happening, so she moved in a bit closer.

"From this moment forth, everyone in Windvale shall be happy! Smile! Be merry! Delight in your existence!" The Queen smiled as she waved her hand in the air, creating a blue glow of ice and snow around it.

Alma watched as the butcher, Mr. Pederson, stepped out of the crowd. He took a knee in front of her, removing his winter hat as he did.

"What is it, my subject?" The Queen asked.

Pederson looked up to meet The Queen's gaze. "My lordship. I haven't had game through these woods in ages. Each day we venture further and further into the tundra, searching for wildlife. How do you expect us to smile more with empty bellies?"

The queen stepped forward from the fountain to stand in front of Pederson. She held his chin in her hand, smiling down at him. Gently, she caressed his bearded cheek with the back of her hand. Mr. Pederson seemed uneased yet relaxed at the same time.

"I see. Perhaps you did not hear my words; were they unclear? I demand that everyone be happy!" The Queen screamed as she floated once more in front of Mr. Pederson. "Unhappy? Are you not finding food? Are you not eating at all? I'm sure you are. Look at you! You oafish, over-bloated buffoon! What do you take me for?"

Mr. Pederson stood up, gripping his hat in his hands nervously. "I meant nothing by it, m'lady! Swear!"

A smirk twisted onto The Queen's face. "So be it. I have told you what to do. My instructions are simple. Now, I shall demonstrate the consequences!"

The queen waved her hand over Mr. Pederson's face. He quickly screamed as he reached for his face. Alma tried to see what had happened to the poor man. As Pederson writhed around on the snow, the townsfolk watched in horror. Slowly, Pederson dropped his hands from his face to retrieve his hat from the snow. Several onlookers in the crowd fainted. The gasp exhaled from the rest of the group made Alma move closer to see. Mr. Pederson's eyes were now glazed in ice! It took everything she had to not scream. There they were, clear as day! Grey and blue, frozen over with ice! She couldn't believe it.

"That was my warning. Should I find any of you are not in absolute delight, frowning, or complaining, I will inflict the same consequence upon you!"

Another town member stepped forward. This time, it was Mrs. Birk. "How exactly will you know, my Queen?"

The evil queen smirked. "Oh, I'll have my eyes. If that fails me, I'll be able to watch you with some help."

She waved her hand in the air across the open field beside her. Dozens of snowmen began to form.

"This is absolutely insane! You cannot do this!" Mrs. Birk shrieked.

With the flick of a wrist and a slight smirk, Mrs. Birk received the same fate as Mr. Pederson. The process seemed painful as she writhed on the floor in agony. Alma glanced over at Mr. Pederson, who was now standing back in line with the townsfolk with a smile ear to ear. His eyes, now an empty hallow full of reflective ice, placing his expression in a somewhat uneasy tone. Alma dashed off to her home at once and closed the door behind her.

As time passed, Alma grew a little older. She also became more adjusted to the new lifestyle. In town, people would pass her by with the largest of smiles. It was obvious which of those scowled, even for a slight moment. Their eyes were replaced with reflective sheets of ice. The ghostly hollow void that once was a beautiful set of eyes sat eerily centered on various faces of the townsfolk. Overall, Alma was glad the Queen hadn't killed them. Things could have been worse. Much, much worse, in fact.

As Alma passed by Mr. Pederson's butcher shop, she peered inside to see what she could see. Beyond the doorway, a dark shop sat ahead of her. The counter was covered in strange meats, while other cuts hung from the various hooks on the walls. Mr. Pederson must have been in the back, as the storefront was empty. Alma decided to step inside to take a better look. The smell was off. There was something about this meat that was not the traditional smell of venison or boar. This was a whole new stench.

"Alma, dear! Welcome to my happy little store! Can I help you with any wonderful selections of meat today?" Mr. Pederson called out as he emerged from the shop's rear, carrying a large slab of prime cuts with him.

Alma backed away slightly, trying to maintain her false smile. "Oh, no, thank you. I just wanted to stop in and say hello."

"Shame about your father and all. Oh well! Would you like some of this meat for the road?" Mr. Pederson said as he gestured his armful of meat at her.

Alma took another step backward toward the door. "Oh, no. I'm fine."

"Cheer up, sweetie. I'm sure your father is with us right now. He'd be proud of the young lady you've become."

Alma thought about the word choices of Mr. Pederson but quickly brushed it off. The memory of losing her father began to trouble her mind, and she didn't need to be seen upset in town. She wiped away a quick tear that started to well up in the corner of her eyes and turned to face the cold outside. She was nearly knocked over by one of the Queen's patrolmen.

"Oh, sorry there!" Alma said, picking herself up with a smile.

The snowman leaned in. The coal for its eyes stared daggers into Alma, practically reading her soul. She almost believed they could read her soul at one point. Without a word, the patrolman began its route once more, gliding gracefully through the snow. The world she knew as a child was becoming less and less what she knew, fading into a memory of times she would never regain.

Her boyfriend, Hansel, waived to her from the doorstep of her home as she returned.

"Alma, sweetie! What a great day, right?" Hansel exclaimed as he picked her up in his arms. "It's almost magical!"

Alma tried to hide her sarcastic smirk before replying. "Whoopie, magical!"

Hansel's expression changed. "Hey, hey now. Don't do that! You know what they'll do to you, right?" Hansel shifted from his slightly serious expression back to a smile. He erupted with a boast of laughter before continuing. "You'll have a great day, that's for sure. So buck up, kiddo!"

Alma hated how fake this town was. She was tired of seeing the dead, void-filled eye sockets of her friends and neighbors. Those that hadn't been converted were living in such fear that they were shells of their former selves. She had been planning to leave ever since her father unexpectedly passed away a few weeks ago. There was nothing for her in this town. Nothing that is, except perhaps Hansel. He could be convinced to flee with her, indeed.

Alma quickly took Hansel by the arm and pulled him into her home. The walls were still adorned with hunting trinkets and trophies from her father. He used to hunt with Mr. Pederson until he fell too ill. Hansel was pulled further into the home, deeper toward the kitchen near the fireplace. Alma quickly lit a roaring fire, glancing around to ensure the coast was clear.

"Ok, listen. I have a plan to get out of here," Alma whispered under the crackling of the firelogs.

Hansel dropped the smirk from his face. "You're kidding me. You want to risk leaving?"

Alma paused momentarily. "I don't think anyone has tried. They're too afraid to. And if they did make it, we'd likely never know, right?"

"Right."

"So, what if we packed a small number of rations and headed out of town. We don't stop running until we see beautiful hills of grass, flowers, and trees."

Hansel smiled at that thought. It was one of the first times he'd worn a genuine smile in a long time. "I think we could do it."

Alma used the dirt on the floor to map out their route. She detailed to Hansel that they would travel on foot. If a horse made a noise, they'd surely be captured. Hansel agreed to that. The plan seemed to make sense as Alma went on. The two of them would leave in the cover of night, tonight. A small bag would be packed for each, nothing metallic. They wanted to ensure stealth was on their side. If any of these patrolmen heard them, frankly, they'd be done for.

Alma and Hansel broke up their plans, quickly rubbing out the floor of anything that could incriminate them should they be captured.

"Ok, I'll meet you near the back of the butcher shop. We'd need to run from there to the main gates. There's barely any cover," Hansel asserted. "We'd have to run as fast as we can. After we're past the gates, we'll dash into the woods for cover."

Alma nodded. This was going to work; she was sure of it. She gave Hansel a final hug before plans were in motion. He set foot out of her door with the most enormous smile on his face. Usually, this would be suspicious. However, in these times, it was just what they needed. His genuine smile and happy demeanor would undoubtedly blend in with the falsities of this town. Alma took a small nap to prepare her body for the grueling journey through ice and snow ahead.

As she awoke, the world was a bit quieter. The town has gone to rest for the evening. She peered out of her door slowly as she noticed the stillness of the night. The sky was black, covered in overcast created by the Evil Queen. A gentle snowfall drifted through the atmosphere, coating the ground on a fresh layer of powder. Quietly, she exited her home, closing the door gently behind her. Taking one last hard look at the structure, she shook out the memories attached to it, pushing herself to move along in the shadows across town.

Alma passed one house, then another. Each one seemed more manageable than the last. The Snow Patrolmen were clearly busy somewhere else. Either they were engaged, or she was just lucky. Swiftly, Alma dashed toward the next home, crouching below an open window. Taking great care to not make a sound as she crawled on hands and knees around the opening, she quietly moved to the opposite side of the home. Her hands now stinging from the cold, frozen snow. She clenched her fists for a moment, knowing time was a fleeting gift. She needed to hurry along to the butcher shop.

Rounding the corner, Alma's heart skipped several beats! One of the Queen's patrol passed directly in front of her. Their snowman bases skidding gently across the fresh powder. They didn't seem to notice her as she relaxed her body against the building. Alma waited a few more moments to ensure the patrol was long out of her sight. She was about to make a mad dash across the main road toward the butcher shop. She'd use the fountain for cover if needed but wanted to make the sprint in one movement.

Alma felt as if she'd been running for hours as she tore across the open road. Crouching, she quickly and swiftly made it to the fountain. Hastily glancing around, Alma checked around for anybody in sight before moving toward the other side of the road. As Alma made it across the two buildings' threshold, she dove for cover behind several barrels. She squinted her eyes tightly, hoping nobody had seen her.

"Oh god, oh god, oh god," she muttered under her breath while trying to breathe normally again.

Peering slightly over the barrels, she glanced down the main road. Once again, as before, it remained empty and quiet. The darkness helped paint an eerie shadow across her once beautiful home in the distance. Her moment of relief was jolted out of her as she felt a hand on her shoulder and another across her mouth as she tried to scream.

"Shh, calm down. It's me!" Hansel grunted through his teeth, trying to be as quiet as possible.

Alma felt a wash of relief over her body as she saw her true love. She gazed into his beautiful dragon scale green eyes. She could still see the fierceness within them, even in the blanket of nightfall.

"Ok, let's move," Alma said, with Hansel nodding in agreement.

The two gently moved from building to building, making their way to the end of the row. Each dash across the open air was no less terrifying than the last. Alma could hear her heartbeat in her head as she rushed across each structure. Soon, they were upon the last building on the left.

"Butcher shop," Hansel whispered as he pointed to the front of the building.

The two of them swiftly moved along the side of the wall, pressing their bodies as close as possible. Inch by inch, the two crept closer and closer to the end of the shop. As they reached the corner, Hansel peered around.

"Clear. You ready?" He asked.

"Ready."

Hansel tightened up the straps to his pack. He knew the two of them were about to sprint to their finish line. Ahead, he could see the gates practically glowing. Hansel gripped Alma's hand and stepped out into the open road. He glanced back to Alma one last time, who shot him a slight smile before the two of them made a mad dash for the gate, hand in hand.

Alma spotted that the shop to the butchers was ajar but paid no mind to it to keep up with Hansel. He was much stronger and faster than she was, practically dragging her along. The gates grew closer and closer, and they ran. Alma could almost picture the flowing rivers, the songbirds chirping, and the children's laughter. She began to run harder than ever before, inspired by her thoughts.

As the two approached the gates, they saw they were still clear! Hansel pushed himself even harder, yanking Alma along for the ride. They passed under the arches of the kingdom entrance into the wooded area beyond. Hansel ran several meters from the trail until he felt the coast was clear. He slowly let go of Alma's hand, leaning against a tree to collect himself. Alma decided to lay on her back and catch her breath. Her heart was pounding so hard.

As they recovered, Hansel felt uneased. Something didn't feel right. He shook the feeling off and grabbed Alma's hand, moving along in the wood line toward the edge of the Queen's reach. Alma began to suspect they were not alone in the woods, either. She continually glanced around at every angle and bend in the dark woods for the hint of something moving. Nothing was out there. She focused her attention forward to see the trees beginning to clear ahead.

"We've made it, Alma! We've made it!" Hansel cheered as he stopped at the edge of the woodline.

Alma stepped forward slightly to see what Hansel was able to see. Ahead of her lie the edge of the snowline, just meters ahead! It was only in reach. Beyond that, she could see darkness on the ground.

"Grass!" Alma exclaimed. "I see grass!"

Hansel smiled at her. She looked deep into his piercing green eyes as he gazed into her large blue ones.

"Look up."

Alma adjusted her gaze to the sky. She wandered around in dismay and wonder as she was able to see the stars for the first time in ages. All the constellations, the galaxies, the heavens! They were there for Alma to take in. She held her arms out as if to reach for the stars herself. She felt a warm glow wash over her as she wiped away several tears that had formed. Alma could hear the hoot of an owl and the buzzing of insects. The sound of the buzzing grew louder and louder. She turned to face Hansel. As she looked upon his face, something was wrong. His once beautiful green eyes were now replaced by hallow, reflective ice shards.

"Not the bees!" Alma screamed as she saw crystalline wasps float away from Hansel.

She immediately went to her lover.

"You see, my dear? I have eyes all over. You cannot escape my grasp," Hansel said.

"I don't understand!" Alma replied, shaking Hansel.

"My eyes, loyal subject. Did you think you'd go unnoticed?" Hansel replied.

From behind several trees, dozens of townsfolk, each with their eyes encased in frozen sheets of ice, stepped into view.

"NO! No!" Alma cried out as she was subdued by Hansel and the others.

The following day, the village resumed its everyday hustle and bustle. The butcher was laying out his freshest cuts while the tailor stitched trousers for the youngsters. The town square was busier than ever before as Alma stepped into the crowded marketplace to purchase goods for the home she and Hansel shared. She walked to the merchant, buying spices to season her stew for the evening.

"What a wonderful day it is!" Alma said, paying for her goods.

"Yes, it really, truly is, isn't it?" the shopkeeper replied.

As Alma collected her purchase, the shopkeeper tried his best to not stare too hard into the icy, cold eyes that sat in Alma's skull. The reflection of his face staring back at him as a reminder that, in fact, the Queen is always watching. Her eyes are everywhere.

How did this come about?

Well, this one is quite simple. Dystopian Ink put out a request for authors to submit a short story, around two to four thousand words centered around fractured fairy tales, Brother's Grimm and the like. Let me be clear: I've never written dystopian. The closest I get is Fubar and that's still a far cry from the Hunger Games.

I jokingly wrote a reply simply making the joke, "Your government wants to know: Do you want to build a snowman?" It was a play on the popular kids' movie, obviously. While I couldn't write about those characters, I dove into Hans Christian Andersen's Ice Queen tale. I went to work right away after getting positive feedback from everyone.

I went through a lousy first draft. It was too much like the most recent cartoon, and not enough dystopia. I regrouped, rethought, and put together what you just finished reading. It was fun. If Dystopian Ink has me back a second time, I'd love the challenge to write out of my element.

Harry Carpenter

About the Author

Harry Carpenter, writer of "Tales from an Ex-Husband" and the "Fubar" series, is a fan of horror, science fiction, and suspense. Born in Baltimore, Maryland, a city full of illustrious authors and performers, Harry began writing in elementary school. He formally pursued his passion, releasing his first book "Tales From An Ex-Husband" in 2019.

Harry has since won the "Best Short Short Story" award from the Veteran's Administration writing contest and was featured as the bestselling author in local book stores.

Using his experiences in the United States Army, various retail and fast food establishments, childhood encounters, and chaotic first marriage, he has developed a mind for creativity.

He is a huge fan of cats, video games, and quirky science fiction and horror movies. He also films an internet web series called "The Web-Pool" on YouTube, as well as volunteers with the "Charm City Ghostbusters," a charity organization out of Baltimore who, as the name dictates, dress as the Ghostbusters 1984 movie.

Harry now lives in Baltimore with his wife and cats.

Other works by Harry Carpenter

Tales From An Ex-Husband

Spooky Tales and Scary Things

Fubar: Blackout

Memoirs of a Crazed Mind

Fubar: Out of Element

Brain Dump

Works Featuring Harry Carpenter

Once Upon a Dystopia

Made in the USA
Middletown, DE
17 August 2021